Ardor

ARDOR

a novel of enchantment

LILY PRIOR

ecco

An Imprint of HarperCollins*Publishers*

HarperCollins books may be purchased for educational, business, or sales promotional use. For information, please write: Special Markets Department, Harper-Collins Publishers Inc., 10 East 53rd Street, New York, NY 10022.

FIRST EDITION

Designed by Amy Hill

Library of Congress Cataloging-in-Publication Data
Prior, Lily, 1966–
Ardor / A Novel of Enchantment Lily Prior. — 1st ed.
p. cm.
ISBN 0-06-052786-2
1. Tuscany (Italy) — Fiction. 2. Missing persons — Fiction. 3. Young women — Fiction. 4. Twins — Fiction.
I. Title.
PS3566.R5767A88 2004
813'.6 — dc22   2003063110

04 05 06 07 08 BVG/RRD 10 9 8 7 6 5 4 3 2 1

For Christopher

Contents

Ardor

It hung in the air over the region that summer, like a cloud, rendering the air thick and pearly. Suspended spangles of gold dust caught the sun and twinkled, causing a pang of longing. Cloying and rose-colored. A perfumed ectoplasm.

"Gardenias," "freesias," "sweet peas," "apple blossom," said the garden lovers, their noses straining to put a label on it.

"Fresh cream," "molten chocolate," "baking bread," "ripe melons," "wild strawberries," said the gourmands, their mouths watering.

"Lust," said the moralists, applying pegs to their noses.

"A saintly emanation," said the sisters of the monastery of Sant'Antonio Abate, giving praise in a special mass officiated over by the bishop.

"Drains," wrote the municipal inspector of environmental health with a flourish on his clipboard.

"Fog," said the meteorologists.

"Fresh air," said the purists.

"Death," said the pessimists.

"Hogwash," said the intellectuals.

"Cholera," said the medics.

Yet it was none of those things. It was ardor, and those that inhaled it, myself included, were stricken.

Characters

Fernanda Ponderosa, *the woman*

Oscar, *the monkey*

Sole and Luna, *the monkey's babies*

Olga, *the turtle (has seven babies: Evangelista, Carla, Debora, Cressida, Dafne, Manon, and Lilla)*

Raffaello di Porzio, *the telegram delivery boy, eleventh precinct*

Vasco, *foreman of the Grossi removal company*

Signora Vasco, *Vasco's wife*

Glauco Pancio, *one of the Grossi removal operatives*

Borrelli, *the bar steward on the* Santa Luigia

Maria Grazia, *my cousin*

Arcadio Carnabuci, *the olive grower*

Concetta Crocetta, *the district nurse*

Myself, Gezabel, *the District Health Authority mule*

Fedra Brini, *the cobweb knitter*

Priscilla Carnabuci, *Arcadio's mother (deceased)*

Remo Carnabuci, *Arcadio's father (deceased)*

Max, *Arcadio's dog*

Amelberga Fidotti, *the draper's assistant*

Speranza Patti, *the church organist, and town librarian*

Teresa Marta, *the blind carpet weaver, and her deaf husband,*
  Berardo
Malco Beato, *chorister, dies of embolism*
Padre Arcangelo, *the parish priest*
Ambrogio Bufaletti, *truck driver*
Irina Biancardi, *ambulance driver*
Gianluigi Pupini, *paramedic*
Maria Calenda, *cheese maker and pig keeper to the house of*
  Castorini
Silvana Castorini (née Ponderosa), *Fernanda Ponderosa's twin*
  sister
Fidelio Castorini, *Silvana's husband, Fernanda's brother-in-law*
Primo Castorini, *the pork butcher, Fidelio's younger brother*
Perdita Castorini, *mother of Fidelio and Primo*
Pucillo's Pork Factory, *archrival of the Happy Pig*
The widow Filippucci, *one of Primo Castorini's lady friends*
The band of thieves known as the Nellinos, and their dog,
  Fausto
Neddo, *the regional hermit*
Sancio, *the Castorini family mule*
Belinda Fondi, *gives birth to an angel*
Romeo Fondi, *Belinda's husband*
Serafino Fondi, *the baby angel*
Felice, Emilio, and Prospero Fondi, *future offspring of Belinda*
  and Romeo
Dr. Amilcare Croce, *the doctor*
The widow Maddaloni
Don Dino Maddaloni, *proprietor of the Maddaloni Funeral Home*
  and Mafia boss
Pomilio, Prisco, Pirro, Malco, Ivano, and Gaddo Maddaloni,
  Don Dino's six sons

Selmo and Narno Maddaloni, *Don Dino's cousins*

Franco Laudato, *painter and handyman*

Luigi Bordino, *the baker*

Gloriana Bordino, *Luigi's wife (deceased)*

Melchiore Bordino, *the baker's son (a pastry cook)*

Susanna Bordino, *Melchiore's wife*

Old Luigi Bordino, *the current Luigi's father*

Manfredi Bordino, *Luigi's grandfather*

Gerberto Nicoletto, *melon farmer*

Filiberto Carofalo, *dairy farmer*

Sebastiano Monfregola, *the barber*

Policarpo Pinto, *the rat catcher*

Luca Carluccio, *the shoemaker*

Carlotta Bolletta, *night nurse at the infirmary*

Signor Alberto Cocozza, *of the Environmental Health and
   Sanitation Department*

The sisters Gobbi, *famous for their facial hair*

Arturo Bassiano, *vendor of lottery tickets*

Carmelo Sorbillo, *the unreliable postman*

Giuseppe Mormile, *Amilcare Croce's nearest neighbor*

Immacolata Mormile, *Giuseppe's wife*

Ardor

Prologue

She must have had a premonition of the tragedy, for when the boy brought the telegram, he found the house boarded up and Fernanda Ponderosa already gone. Raffaello di Porzio could tell from the feel of the wire that it contained bad news. As he stood on the deserted porch, holding it in his palm, the burden of the misery it contained descended upon him, and he could scarcely stagger down the steps under the weight of it.

Already the paradise garden, which was famous throughout the island, had assumed a mantle of abandoned beauty. In the two hours since her departure, every one of the three hundred varieties of orchids had wilted. The cascades of velvet roses had withered, as had the sweet peas, the gardenias, and the tender freesias. The baby peaches had shriveled, and the lawns, once green and lush and perfect as a maharaja's carpet, had become parched. No longer did the scents of orange blossom and lavender and honeysuckle pervade the air; now there was the stench of rotting and decay. The butterflies, once so plentiful, had vanished along with the bees that used to suckle so happily at the blooms. The statue of the goddess Aphrodite had also disappeared, leaving a bare patch of earth that wriggled with wood lice and worms, and the tinkling fountain now played the sound of weeping, not laughter.

Raffaello di Porzio shivered. The air of gloom cast a cold shadow over the gardens even though the sun was at its highest. Nevertheless, gathering his strength, he set off in pursuit of her, careering through the steep cobbled streets on his bicycle, seized by a feeling of panic and by the need to do his duty.

Although Raffaello di Porzio never found her, Fernanda Ponderosa was eventually traced to the offices of the Grandi Traghetti, where she sat like a queen on the dock surrounded by more of her possessions than was prudent. A cast-iron bathtub that had been in her family for nine generations sat there wearing the same tight expression as Fernanda Ponderosa herself: of dread and determination. Five men had carried it there, under the direction of the foreman, Vasco, the salt of their sweat plopping through the flimsy planking and combining with the ocean swell.

Yet in vain did Glauco Pancio sustain the rupture, one more tragedy on a day of tragedies, for the bathtub defeated them all, and with a shudder that seemed human, followed by a mighty splintering as though caused by an ogre wielding a giant ax, the bathtub fell through the rotting planks. It sank majestically down to the ocean floor, where it landed with a dull thud on the sand to the openmouthed astonishment of the parrot fish and the dismay of the limpets clinging quietly to the legs of the jetty.

It was a miracle that Fernanda Ponderosa remained dry, and although she affected not to have noticed it, she regarded the submersion of the bathtub as another omen. The removal men, taking their cue from her, saw it would seem indelicate to mention it. It occurred to no one to mount a rescue operation. The bathtub that for three hundred years had purified her illustrious forebears, cleansing from them the gore of battle, the mucus of childbirth, the perspiration of lovers, was now reduced to laundering the less punctilious mermaids of the Marina Grande.

Fernanda Ponderosa looked around with alarm at her other goods and chattels, half expecting those remaining to become submerged under the foaming sea. She regarded herself as the premature victim of a shipwreck although she was still technically on dry land. The gilded cage containing her lugubrious monkey, Oscar, was poised on the edge of the splintered precipice, and though he feigned unconcern, his tiny toes were curled up in a gesture of terror that he could not hide from Fernanda Ponderosa. The sailor suit, in which she had carefully dressed him that morning in preparation for the voyage, was soaked by the spray and by his secret tears.

She moved the cage to what appeared to be a place of safety, and reaching into her bag, she handed the monkey through the bars a linen handkerchief edged with fine lace with which he blotted himself dry. He paid particular attention to the areas behind his ears, which were prone to the development of a fungus, to the spaces between his toes, which were slowly beginning to unfurl now that the initial danger was past, and to his rumpled suit, now sadly reduced from the pristine condition in which he had left the house only a short time before. The monkey was nothing if not methodical.

The great oak chests containing linens and laces blocked the approach to the waterside. Under the direction of the laconic Vasco, who had come late to removals—he had devoted his young life to the building of barricades—the men had abandoned her goods with the intricate inattention of those who prepare obstacle races. Cast onto the dock like the jumble of a bad dream was a wooden rocking horse with a mane of real hair, the life-size marble statue of the goddess Aphrodite, which Raffaello di Porzio had already noted as being missing from the gardens, a chaise longue, a spiral staircase, family portraits of the noble house of Ponderosa, a glass tank containing the turtle Olga and her seven coin-size babies, a weathervane, a baptismal font dating from the time of the first Crusades, a selection of hatboxes, a grand piano, the mounted head of a unicorn, a stuffed pygmy hippopotamus in a display cabinet, a harp supported by carved wooden angels, a heavy oak crib, a grandfather clock, a nest of galvanized buckets, an elephant's-foot umbrella stand, copper pans, a feather bed, an American-style refrigerator stocked for the journey, tennis rackets, a crystal chandelier, a banana tree, and finally a valise containing gold ingots and precious jewels.

This selection was by no means the entire contents of the house, nor indeed the most precious, but when she had woken that morning her heart gripped by the presentiment of calamity, she had taken with her only those things that she would have rescued in the event of a fire. When she moved, and she moved often, she took the things that came first into her hands and that way avoided the agonies of decision-making at a time when life and death hung in the balance.

Although the removal was incomplete, the need to conduct Glauco Pancio to the infirmary became pressing. He was splayed out on a pallet, clutching his nether regions, and groaning pitifully. Fernanda Ponderosa waved the removal men away like flies (it had become impossible for them to do anything outside of the group, and when one went, the rest had to follow) and was left feeling outnumbered by the ranks of her own possessions, which seemed to have taken on a different character now that they were out of the house, in the sunshine on the quay, indelicately exposed to public view.

The tourists on package holidays with little more than a suitcase each and an armful of tacky mementos regarded her with hostility for taking up so much space, and low-pitched mutterings reached her ears, bringing a flush of annoyance to her cheeks. A young man in a uniform appeared with a clipboard and indicated in official jargon that Fernanda Ponderosa could expect to be invoiced by the Grandi Traghetti for the damage caused to the public access areas. But worse was yet to come.

En route to the infirmary, Vasco, who was far from competent behind the wheel of a truck, failed to spot Raffaello di Porzio turning in from the Via della Fortuna, still waving the telegram in his fist and calling upon Fernanda Ponderosa to appear. Many agreed it was a blessing that Raffaello di Porzio died instantly as a result of the impact. Vasco was not so lucky. After flying through the air for three blocks he landed on his head on the roof of the military headquarters and was then peppered with bullets by an overzealous sentry who mistook him for a terrorist.

Although his dented head, and his body full of holes like a colander, were patched up by the finest surgeons the island had to offer, Vasco's mind was never recovered. Signora Vasco liked to think that it was still in trajectory, and while her husband's living corpse lay motionless in a hammock, she consoled herself with the belief that his mind was orbiting the earth.

The telegram, too, was never recovered. It was not discovered in the grasp of Raffaello di Porzio, and indeed when the closed fists of the body were prized open, they were found to contain nothing but frozen teardrops, which his mother collected with care and kept forever in a jar in her icebox. Whatever had happened to it, no trace of the telegram was ever seen again, and as a result Fernanda Ponderosa made the voyage on the strength of her intuition alone. An intuition that, it has to be said, she never doubted for a moment, and according to which she regulated the rhythm of her life.

In the cacophony of bugles and sirens that marked the worst road traffic accident the town could remember, a band of thieves took advantage of the uproar and stole away a number of Fernanda Ponderosa's goods from the quayside. Only later when the *Santa Luigia* had finally docked and the porters began loading the cargo did she discover the theft, and by then there was nothing she could do about it. Once she had ascertained that Oscar and Olga and her seven babies were safe, she was able to accept the robbery with a calm she dug down deep for. Besides, she reasoned that this was a passing sorrow compared to that which she knew was waiting to confront her at her journey's end. She had, after all, never liked the portraits; the spiral staircase was probably not going to be of much use to her; and she had never approved of her ancestors' tendency toward big-game hunting. She supervised the loading of what remained and then took her place at the prow.

When the ferry finally sailed, she did not give one backward glance to the island paradise she was leaving forever. She made a policy of never looking back. Instead she looked out to sea, to the school of acrobatic dolphins, hundreds strong, dancing in the glittering waters, and to the enormous octopus being landed with difficulty on the deck by a schoolboy with a fishing rod.

On land, her departure was greeted by many with relief. The morning's events had reinforced her reputation as a jinx, and the Vasco and di Porzio families, despite their grief, felt it prudent to offer their friends a little wine and a few almond cakes in celebration of her going.

Throughout the two days and nights of the passage, Fernanda Ponderosa refused to take any rest, and neither would she abandon her vantage point at the prow of the ship. She stood like a figurehead, wrapped in a black seafarer's cape, which billowed out behind her in the wind. She seemed a sinister apparition to the other passengers, mostly commercial travelers with suitcases full of rubber gloves, hairpieces, or surgical prostheses.

Was she a ghost? they asked Borrelli, the bar steward, who boosted his sales with blood-chilling lies concerning Fernanda Ponderosa, which left the customers in need of copious amounts of bottled courage to return to their cabins. Yet Fernanda Ponderosa was guilty of nothing more sinister than urging the vessel onward, and trying in vain to understand the cause of the grief in her heart.

Eventually the *Santa Luigia* reached port, and Fernanda Ponderosa, the monkey, the family of turtles, and the goods that remained were bundled rudely onto another dock, this one on the mainland, far away from home. They made a forlorn little group, particularly when the heavens opened, and they found themselves submersed in a pool of water that lent them the picturesque aspect of a fountain. The turtles didn't mind the damp, but the monkey hated it, and he was obliged to blot himself once more with the handkerchief, which had only just dried out.

I know all of this because, by an amazing coincidence, my cousin Maria Grazia was herself being transported on the *Santa Luigia,* and she saw *firsthand* everything that happened.

part one

SOWING

CHAPTER ONE

The man who was responsible for this whole mix-up was our own Arcadio Carnabuci, the olive grower. Demoralized by the rejection he had suffered from every woman he had approached in the region, and exhausted by his debilitating loneliness, he grew desperate. At precisely the moment this happened, there was a knock on the door and he was seduced by the glib patter of a passing peddler. Within seconds he had purchased at great expense a handful of seeds the gypsy guaranteed would bring him love.

Gleefully the peddler pocketed the cash and ran off before the olive grower could change his mind. But he need not have worried. Arcadio Carnabuci was delighted with his purchase and couldn't wait to change his life. Nobody could have predicted the way things would turn out, but I will faithfully record it all in these pages, for I myself was intimately involved with everything that happened.

Yes, responding to the irresistible surge of nature, Arcadio Carnabuci sowed the seeds of his love early in the spring, when the short days of fleeting February were hurrying into March, and already the earth was coming alive. Mists hung around the skirts of the hills like tulle, and on the plains tiny figures became visible, muffled against the cold, sowing the crops where the snow had melted.

Arcadio Carnabuci spent the daylight hours on the rungs of a ladder, pruning the olive trees that had been in the care of his family for one thousand years. But his mind was not on his olives. No. It was on love.

In the crisp air that clouded with his breath, he could feel the tension, taut like the twigs that snapped beneath his knife. Overnight, the almond trees poured forth their blossoms. Not to be outdone, the cherry trees followed; so, too, did the persimmons, the chestnuts, and the pomegranates. The sticky buds on the willows gave forth curly catkins, and the meadows exploded into a blaze of spring flowers: lily of the valley, dwarf narcissi, bluebells, crocuses, and irises formed a carpet of dazzling color. Wild asparagus and sweet-smelling herbs perfumed the newborn air, and up on the mountains, rhododendrons bloomed.

Arcadio Carnabuci could feel the earth's energy through the soles of his stout boots. This effervescence bubbled up into his legs and made him dance in spite of himself.

"Look, I'm dancing," he cried to no one in particular, all the more amazed because he had never danced a step in his life before. And he started to laugh.

"I'm dancing."

And so he was. Slowly at first, but as his confidence grew, he threw himself into the rhythm of the dance. His arms joined in; his feet, usually leaden, became weightless. They bounced off the hardened earth and soared into the air. He dipped and dived like a swallow. He gyrated his hips. He flung his head about.

Those that saw him turned up their coat collars and examined their mittens to cover their embarrassment. Arcadio Carnabuci, always strange, was growing stranger. That day my colleague Concetta Crocetta, the district nurse, received seven separate reports calling for Arcadio Carnabuci to be interred in the *manicomio* at Cascia for the benefit of all in the region. Yet when we trotted past the olive grove to witness Arcadio Carnabuci's antics, we saw it was nothing more than high spirits connected with the coming of spring. Smiling indulgently, she gave me a tap with her little heel to encourage me. Back then she was never rough with my tender flanks, and we set off again for home.

The impulse that was tickling away at Arcadio Carnabuci was not confined to himself and the plants. No. Animals felt it, too. The spiders in their spangled webs yearned for love and spun sonnets of a fragile and unbearable beauty, glazed with tears of dew. Scorpions in dark corners clipped their castanets in courtship, then curled up in pairs in discarded shoes, snug as bugs. The mice in the rafters scurried about gathering wisps of stolen cotton, torn paper, and bits of fluff and formed them into cozy nests from which they subsequently brought forth blind babies the size of peas. The humble newts in the waterspout sung out in deep voices. The frogs and the toads joined in with them, and soon a chorus of magical croaking was filling the air. The music they made was so beautiful it made those that heard it weep and yearn for the life of an amphibian so they could unlock the secret of the song. Already the beady-eyed blackbirds were busily building their nests, watched slyly by the cuckoos, who were broadcasting the news, for those that didn't already know it: spring had sprung. Deep in the oak woods, the wild boar grunted his serenade, while, in the sty, his domestic cousins spooned. Deer frolicked, hares chased. High up in the mountains the wolf howled his suit, and the shy brown bears hugged in their caves.

Arcadio Carnabuci could not help but succumb to the rosy glow that wrapped itself around the region, and his loins hummed with a cruel expectation that in his lonely circumstances he could do little to fulfill. But he had faith in his love seeds, and in this fertile climate their promise would surely come to fruition.

It was then that he sowed them. He picked the moment with care. In the watery sunlight, frail but willing. Under glass. To keep them warm. They were more beans than seeds. Pleasantly plump, and a palish pink in color. Little crescent moons. He could feel a tingling in the beans; like jumping beans, they possessed the same energy as everything else around him. He held them for a while in the palm of his hand, familiarizing himself with them, scrutinizing them through his half-moon glasses, behind which his eyes seemed enormous, and every pore and hair follicle was magnified a thousand times. Even the beans could feel the strength of his hope, and the plucky little creatures were determined not to disappoint him.

He tucked them up under the soil, as though tucking his mistress into bed. They were invested with the weight of so many hopes and dreams, little trickles, squiggles of beauty, and longing, trailing ripples of excitement. His slow movements were a symphony. In his hands, the fleshy spades of a farmer, the beans knew they were safe. The pads of his fingers, broad but gentle, pressed upon them, and in the sudden darkness and peaty warmth they fell asleep.

Then, like the blackbirds in the hedgerows, like the mice under the eaves, Arcadio Carnabuci began to feather his nest. His bachelor home boasted few comforts. The stains on the walls cried out to him. The sun-bleached curtains embarrassed him. He began to clean. He swept up the piles of dust with a broom that had itself grown dusty. He startled the mice by reaching into long-forgotten corners that had ceased to belong to him.

After many years he finally relented and allowed Fedra Brini into the house to gather the cobwebs she needed for knitting her sails. She was the only sailmaker in this landlocked region, and her sails were sent to the shores of the Adriatic, where they were highly prized among the fishermen for their fineness and durability. She regularly stripped all the other houses in the district, and the cobwebs of Arcadio Carnabuci left unharvested for so long were magnificent, like something from a fairy tale.

Fedra Brini was ecstatic, the spiders less so. The heritage of generations was lost in a few deft swipes of her pruning hook. Folklore, legend, the family tree inscribed in curly calligraphic script, works of great literature, love stories, poetry, mysteries, whodunits, even recipes and crossword puzzles, and to add injury to insult, one of the young spiders lost a leg in Fedra's attack, for which Arcadio Carnabuci was never forgiven. All was swept up and carried off in a little linen sack on the back of the destroyer. It was a terrible day.

Fedra Brini, so full of joy, like a brimming jug, she could no longer contain it. Such sumptuous webs, she started telling people. Hadn't been touched since the death of Priscilla Carnabuci, Arcadio's mother, twenty-two years before. But why had Arcadio Carnabuci, who had resisted her requests for so long, finally given in? No one could say for sure. But clearly the olive grower was up to something, and Fedra, who luxuriated in the warm rays of her neighbors' notice, did her best to fuel the fires of their curiosity.

Fanning the flames further, the very same olive grower showed up one morning in the draper's in the Via Colombo, asking for bedsheets. What could Arcadio Carnabuci want with new bed linen? The eyebrows of Amelberga Fidotti, the draper's sour-faced assistant, immediately formed themselves into question marks. Soon the news was on every pair of lips in the town. It scarcely seemed possible. Or decent. He was a bachelor after all, and one with long teeth at that.

. . .

When he got home, he tried the sheets out on the bed. Just to examine the effect. Not to use, of course. They were almost too magnificent. Shockingly so. Crisp and fresh as fields of new snow. Yet he was troubled. He didn't want to look as though he had tried too hard. He didn't want it to seem that he had tried at all, in truth. Suppose he appeared calculating? Too self-assured? That he had planned the moment instead of allowing it to unfold in an impromptu way. Nevertheless, his worn and graying sheets were a disgrace. Painfully he refolded the new ones, matching the original creases like folding a map, and squeezed them back into the crunchy cellophane wrappers that were wonderful in themselves. He shut them up in a drawer. The next time he got them out would be for her. And he blushed a hot sticky blush that transformed him into a teenager.

Arcadio Carnabuci never doubted for a second that his true love would come. He knew it as a certainty. As surely as the olives appeared on his trees. He could dig around their roots to give them air, fertilize them with dung, prune them, all on the given days set out by his forebears in the great Carnabuci Almanac, yet he knew that whatever he did, there would still be olives. There would be olives growing on the trees long after he would become the fertilizer himself. With the same certainty, he knew she would come.

Arcadio Carnabuci checked on the progress of his seeds hundreds of times a day. He almost wore out the soil in the tray by looking at it. How he willed the slightest shard of green to protrude through the surface! In the mornings, before even emptying his bladder, he would hurry to the windowsill while still bending the wires of his spectacles around the backs of his ears and examine the soil as though panning for gold.

Finally, on a glorious Palm Sunday, a day that would be forever etched on his memory, three proud little protuberances were waiting for him as self-satisfied as schoolchildren who have answered every question correctly in a spelling test. How his heart leapt at the sight of them. He examined them so closely he soon knew the minutest characteristics of each individual specimen. His prayers had been answered. It had to be a sign, on this of all days, that the Lord was with him.

Later that day, when he took up his accustomed place in the church strewn with palm fronds, he did not hold back his thanks for that small miracle. I was then, as now, a complete agnostic and so of course never went to church, but I clearly remember passing by there that morning, and I heard everything. Yes, his glorious baritone resounded with all the force of his passion, welling into a great bubble in the nave that almost raised the roof from its rafters. It outdid the organ, and as much as the prim organist, Speranza Patti, played up to try and drown him out, Arcadio would not be outdone.

Taking their cue from Speranza Patti, the members of the choir inflated their lungs and puffed out their chests and cheeks, looking for everything like the lusty cherubs adorning the frescoes above their heads. They sang out with everything they had, their voices mingling together in one great evangelical soup. Teresa Marta, the blind carpet weaver, sang so fervently that had their been a God in heaven she should by rights have been given her sight back. Fedra Brini gave it her all, so much so that she began to hyperventilate and had to be led outside to breathe into a paper bag; it had been an emotional week for her after all. Malco Beato pounded out the responses as though his life depended upon it, which to a certain extent it did. This stupendous effort was thought by many to be responsible for the embolism he was to suffer later that day, which left the Beato front parlor looking like a war zone. Every last member of the choir was left reeling, dizzy, red-faced, and breathless by the grand finale, which rocked the little church and could easily have triggered an earthquake, yet Arcadio Carnabuci did not even break into a sweat, and his one voice still rose above those of the fifty trained choristers.

Padre Arcangelo was delighted at the strength of Arcadio Carnabuci's zeal at the sacred mysteries, but the other worshipers exchanged glances to show that the olive grower was once again up to his tricks. Those unfortunate enough to be sharing the same pew sidled away fearing for the effect on their eardrums, and sure enough a record number of cases of tinnitus were subsequently reported to Concetta Crocetta, all of them blamed on Arcadio Carnabuci.

CHAPTER TWO

During the following days the precious seedlings stretched and arched their necks and raised their heads above the soil, straining toward the sun that pored rashly through the windows. All work in the olive grove was suspended as Arcadio Carnabuci devoted himself to watching the progress of his plantlets, and as he watched, he spoke words of encouragement, tender phrases, lines of poetry, the language of love.

Arcadio Carnabuci's long-dead father, Remo, took a dim view of his son's neglect of the grove and appeared to him in a dream urging him to return to work, for the olive trees were more important than the individuals born to serve them. But Priscilla, Arcadio's mother, soon entered the dream to point out to her husband that if Arcadio remained a bachelor much longer, there would be no Carnabucis left to tend the grove, or to do anything else. The parents' dispute raged over Arcadio's head and he felt nostalgic for the days of his youth when they were all together in life, a happy family.

When they took to throwing pots at one another and name-calling, Arcadio decided to leave them to it, and pulling the covers over his ears, he replaced them with a dream in which he was serenading his beloved. In the twilight she stood on a balcony, and he, in a magical garden below, was enveloped by the velvety darkness. His rendition of "E lucevan le stelle" was the most perfect performance he had ever given and was accompanied by an orchestra of frog song, and the cantata of the small, shy creatures of the night.

The following morning Arcadio Carnabuci was mildly surprised to find his kitchen in chaos: broken pots were everywhere, egg yolks smeared the walls, jars of preserves were smashed, chairs were upturned. It even appeared that a flour fight had taken place.

His immediate concern was for the safety of his seeds, and his relief was enormous when he found them undisturbed. If anything, they were more lush and verdant than the night before.

Throughout Holy Week the sprouts spurted such growth it seemed incredible. They were growing right before his eyes. If he turned his back for a moment, he could perceive a difference. If he went into town to run some errands, on his return he would see a fresh-formed inch of stalk, or a new little leaf unfurling its tender green flag.

Arcadio Carnabuci was so excited he felt ready to explode. Truthfully, he was a time bomb waiting to go off. He couldn't concentrate on any one thing. A sweat stood out perpetually on his brow. He kept doing stupid things, losing items, putting them in the wrong places. He spent hours looking for his socks only to find them in the refrigerator; the jug of milk stuffed into his coat pocket had curdled into yogurt. His taste buds were confused. He ate a slab of cheese only to discover later it was butter. The liver he fried for his supper was an old slipper.

It was then, too, that the dreams started. Arcadio Carnabuci began to see Fernanda in dreams. The sweetest little ear would appear in the middle of a dream about something else entirely. Or a perfect nose. Just the kind of nose he desired her to have. Small, straight, narrow. Freckles. A scattering of fine freckles evenly distributed over the surface of her luminous skin. Eyes green, deep green, not pale, and ardent like a lake with splashes of sun on it. Her hair particularly distracted him, in dreams, and even when he knew he was awake, he saw it. Twisted into a corn plait, the color of the sunset on a field of wheat. It seemed so close, so real, he could almost reach out and touch it. He knew what it felt like, to the touch. Smooth, like a skein of silk thread warmed by the sun. Sometimes it was flung over his pillow, like a pool of molten gold. He could smell it, like a summer meadow when the grasses and the wildflowers were in bloom and their scent carried on the breeze. But when he reached out to it, it vanished.

As the seedlings developed, the image of Fernanda also came into focus. Arcadio Carnabuci knew her name from the start. It did not come as a surprise. It seemed that he had always known it: Fernanda. It spoke to him from somewhere in a distant past that they had shared, long ago and far away from here. This reinforced his notion of the inevitability of it all. Their coming together at long last was their destiny.

He took to repeating her name over and over like a mantra: Fernanda, Fernanda. Sometimes, when he was feeling a little tipsy after too much wine, or sometimes even without the wine, just when he was feeling joyful and irrepressible, he would couple her name with his own: "Fernanda Carnabuci. Signora Fernanda Carnabuci." How good it sounded. And so right. So natural. He didn't want to tempt fate by mentioning it to anybody else, but he wore it in his heart like a mascot.

He knew all sorts of intimate things about her. He knew the curve of her thighs so well he could draw it with one unfaltering pencil line. His mind when at leisure would unconsciously trace that curve. He worshiped the pale blue network of veins on her inner arms, the tender place that, when he stroked along its length softly with the whisper of a fingertip, would gather her up into a endless line of pleats and make her mew and arch like a cat. Her skin was always cold to the touch, cold and smooth as marble. Just short of the place where her cheeks melted into her hairline, they were crosshatched with downy hair too fine to be described as hair, as delicate as the blush of felt on a ripe peach, and the sight of it made him want to weep. Her long, narrow feet—he loved every one of the tiny bones that composed them. He loved the part of her she was herself less familiar with: her back. The two hinted indentations either side of the base of her spine, the freckles that flecked across her shoulders, the adorable vertebra that became pronounced when she bent over, the aspect her back bore of being younger than her front because it was less looked at. Her succulent breasts startled him every time they came into his mind, tinged with guilt perhaps because he knew he shouldn't be looking at them. Perfect, that was all.

After a night of delirious dreams, her legs entangled with his, the clinging, rich perfume of warm salt bodies released with every rise and fall of the quilt, the air outside the bed cold, strands of her hair lay across his face, stray hairs in his mouth, his arm forming a pillow for her neck. Her almost imperceptible breathing, the only sound in the world just then, made him hold his own breath so terrified was he of waking her and disturbing her. Her mouth, slightly open in repose, plucked a string that connected straight and deep to his loins and set them twanging with pleasure.

Yes, on the morning directly after he had seen this dream, the morning of Easter Sunday, Arcadio Carnabuci, dredging himself reluctantly from the slow, deep, burning sultry beauty of the night, and the heavy fug of sleep, was jarred to reality and shocked to discover miniature fruit dangling from slender tendrils beneath the leaves of his saplings. It was incredible. There had been no hint of them the night before. And here they were. Three of them. Triplets.

They were unlike any fruit he had ever seen. They were the shape of eggplants, only small, so small, and sweet, with a creamy-colored flesh splotched irregularly but charmingly with brown, like the markings of a Friesian cow. And literally as he watched, the fruit swelled. Their little bellies grew rounded and sleek. He couldn't resist touching them ever so gently with the pad of a finger, a touch as light as a blade of grass bowing to the breeze. He was almost certain he heard a giggle coming from the tickled fruit.

Impatiently he waited for the public library to open after Holy Week, for he wanted to find out all he could about the love seeds (the peddler had been cryptically vague when questioned about cultivation, but had made elaborate promises for his seeds and sworn Arcadio Carnabuci wouldn't be disappointed). The first morning of reopening, he was loitering on the steps as Speranza Patti, the church organist who was also the town librarian, arrived at work. She ignored him, hoping he would slink away again, but Arcadio Carnabuci was a persistent man. Although she attempted to shut the heavy door against him, he followed her inside and spent several hours rummaging among the shelves in the section on agronomy and horticulture.

All the while, in some discomfort, Speranza Patti tried to perform her duties while keeping a trembling finger close to the panic button. What on earth could Arcadio Carnabuci want in the public library? He wasn't even a member. She shivered at the thought that they were alone together in the building. Who knew what he was capable of? Anything could happen. Unbeknown to her, Arcadio Carnabuci had his head buried in Lucentini's aged volume of *Exotic Fruits*. He was not a fast reader, and painstakingly he examined each and every page looking for something that resembled his own precious fruits, but when he reached the end, he had found nothing even remotely similar.

With equal care he ploughed his way through every other volume in the section: treatises on beans, encyclopedias of plants, compendiums, digests, dictionaries, directories, handbooks. None bore fruit. His fruit were unique: of a type unknown to botanists and husbandmen. This confirmed what he had already himself suspected: they were little miracles, all his own. His slight feelings of disappointment at his fruitless search were outbalanced by his secret joy at his own fruits' uniqueness and he left the library singing.

At last Speranza Patti was able to relax and enjoy her bread and cheese in peace behind the counter, but she had developed a cramp in her forefinger that took a long time to ease. Word that Arcadio Carnabuci had been skulking in the town library soon circulated, and Speranza Patti was besieged by citizens who demanded to know what he had been doing in there. The library had never had as many visitors as this in a single day. Speranza Patti, now the center of attention, had to admit to feeling rather pleased with herself and played up to the crowd in a way she thought was demanded of her. Soon bizarre rumors went round concerning Arcadio Carnabuci: he was in league with the devil; he was planning to overthrow the town council; he was the cause of the recent earthquake; he was a fugitive on the run from justice; a pirate; a vampire; a eunuch; a secret transvestite.

Back home, oblivious to the wildfire of gossip about him, Arcadio Carnabuci continued to monitor his fruits minute by minute. They rewarded him by developing before his eyes. Fascinated, he watched each minor change: each minuscule swelling in the girth of the three fruits, the trembling variations in hue of the suedey skin. Tenderly he cupped each of them in the palm of his hand to assess their individual weights, taking care so as not to damage them or cause them to drop prematurely from the umbilical stalks that bound them to the parent plants.

He waited with a mixture of patience and anxiety. Of course he was eager to taste the fruit and unleash the forces of the miraculous change that was destined to take place in his life. But he also realized that he should wait until the magic fruits had reached the perfect pitch of ripeness so they would have maximum potency. Arcadio Carnabuci figured he had waited forty years; a few more days wouldn't matter. He not only watched, he inhaled the scent of the fruit, noting subtle gradations in depth and tone, fearful of the least whiff of putrefaction and decay.

The turning of the world had almost stopped for Arcadio Carnabuci. So much now happened between each single tick of the clock. His fruits were everything. There was nothing else.

Then, finally, on the twenty-seventh of April at twenty-five past ten, he knew the time had come. The fruits were perfectly ripe, they had reached the precise moment of ripeness, which his whole life of farming olives had taught him. And so, not a second too early or too late, he garnered his courage, swallowed hard, and plucked them manfully from the supporting stalks.

The little dears had a feel almost human. They were warm, soft, and fleshy. Yet Arcadio Carnabuci could not afford to be sentimental now. With a sharp knife he began to pare them, stripping the thinnest sliver of the cream-and-brown peel away, causing it to curl in a snaking spiral onto the table. The cut fruits released an aroma that almost knocked Arcadio Carnabuci off his feet. It was the smell of vanilla, champagne, longing, marzipan, peaches, smiles, cream, strawberries, raspberries, roses, melting chocolate, lilac, figs, laughter, honeysuckles, kisses, lilies, enchantment, ardor itself.

Then, after so much patience, he could no longer wait, and greedily, lecherously, he crammed the juicy fruits into his mouth, one after the other. His mind could not believe the signals his taste buds were relaying to him through the spaghetti of his senses. It was like a star bursting in his mouth. The taste was fruity, certainly, but unlike any other fruit he had ever tasted. He closed his eyes with the pleasure of it, and rivulets of joy—no, waves, huge breakers of surf—washed over him, saturating him, leaving him weak.

When he had consumed the fruits and licked up every last drop of juice from the table, licked his fingers and the palms of his hands, and his lips and jowls and chin, he felt full to the brim with creaminess and satiation.

Finally, he slumped down into his chair with the vestiges of a smile covering his face. Only later did he feel the calm that crept upon him, and he settled down to wait for what would happen next.

CHAPTER   THREE

While Arcadio Carnabuci sat back and waited, far to the
south Fernanda Ponderosa and her retinue were also waiting,
but for what, nobody knew. Then, quite by chance, the appearance of a truck on the quayside, driven by one Ambrogio
Bufaletti, propelled them onto the next stage in their journey.

Signor Bufaletti licked his lips at the sight of Fernanda Ponderosa; in fact, he was slavering at the mouth, but he was a
businessman first and foremost, and he could not allow his lust
to prevent him from driving a hard bargain. And so protracted
negotiations followed, complicated by the fact that Fernanda
Ponderosa, guided by her instinct alone, did not know where
they were going. She closed her eyes and tried to intuit the
place while Ambrogio Bufaletti rolled his eyes toward the skies
and made the typical gestures of impatience.

In her mind's eye, Fernanda Ponderosa saw a big and naked
man with animal eyes. She smelled the irresistible aroma of
baking bread. She saw meadows of bluebells. She saw pigs,
both the domestic variety and the wild, tusked kind. She heard

their grunts and snorts. And she saw cheese. Which made her sneeze. She saw olive groves climbing over gently rolling hills. She saw hands forming sausages. She felt whispered kisses on the back of her neck. She tasted ham. She saw vines in neat rows. She saw dark oak woods, and then, suddenly, a cemetery.

"Mountains," she said at last. Her voice was deep, almost too deep for a woman, and rich. It was resonant, as if it belonged deep underground. It made every sailor, stevedore, fisherman, and customs official loitering on the dockside stop what he was doing and look in her direction. She felt their notice warming her but did not give the tiniest flicker of acknowledgment.

Ambrogio Bufaletti made no effort to remove his eyes from Fernanda Ponderosa's magnificent breasts.

"So, you want the Himalayas, signora?"

"Just head east, signor," she said with a flash of her dark eyes, "I will navigate."

Ambrogio Bufaletti insisted on being paid an inflated price, in cash, in advance. Only then were the goods loaded aboard the truck, and they set off in search of the mountainous region of Fernanda Ponderosa's imagination. Only then, when Fernanda Ponderosa was out of sight, did the commercial travelers feel it prudent to descend the gangplank, and hauling behind them their heavy suitcases, they set about their business.

So began a journey that was to haunt the monkey's nightmares for years to come. Behind the wheel of the truck, what remained of Ambrogio Bufaletti's patience was blown out the window along with the smoke of his endless cigarettes. He preferred the view of Fernanda Ponderosa to the road ahead of him, and despite her requests that he keep his eyes on the highway, he did not seem able to control them. Where the road meandered in bends, he took a straight line as his path, and the oncoming traffic was forced to divert into the ditches alongside to avoid collision. He careered along at speeds for which his ramshackle vehicle was not designed, and he did not feel concern for the pieces that dropped off and formed a trail in their wake. In towns and in places of congestion he mounted the sidewalk to effect a shortcut around the traffic. In Collesalvetti he plowed through a group of nuns, scattering them like doves. In Ponsacco they were flagged down by an officer of the carabinieri, but Ambrogio Bufaletti refused to stop and jammed his foot on the gas, leaving the officer coughing in a cloud of blue smoke while he radioed for reinforcements. The journey had only just begun and already they were fugitives from justice.

The monkey kept his tiny hands clamped over his face and from time to time emitted plaintive howls that were barely audible above the roar of the laboring engine and the expletives of the driver.

Fernanda Ponderosa also shut her eyes, and Ambrogio Bufaletti was not slow to take advantage by groping her thighs with every movement of the shift stick. This assault she attempted to ignore, but when he grew bolder and reached for her bosoms, she lashed out at him with the nearest object to hand, cracking a tin plate against his skull like a cymbal. In his surprise he struggled to keep control of the truck and narrowly avoided plowing through the barriers of a bridge and plunging into the raging torrent below.

Though he didn't say anything, Ambrogio Bufaletti was not pleased, and the atmosphere within the smoky cab definitely darkened. After this he took to purposefully removing both hands from the steering wheel to increase Fernanda Ponderosa's terror. She controlled her impulse to scream and grabbed the wheel. It was a war of nerves, which Fernanda Ponderosa intended to win.

They crossed and recrossed Florence as Ambrogio Bufaletti repeatedly missed the right turn. The vast groups of Japanese tourists following flag-waving guides were forced to run for cover as the truck careered between their ranks, and blurred images of a grim-expressioned Fernanda Ponderosa were snapped by thousands of high-speed telephoto lenses. The Duomo itself became dizzy as the battered truck circled it for the twentieth time. The Fontana di Nettuno, the Palazzo Vecchio, the Davide, the Uffizi, the Arno, all whirled past at dangerous speeds in this nightmarish sight-seeing tour. And finally they were out and on their way again, leaving the city's treasures and tourists to regroup themselves as best they could.

After many hours and many miles, it seemed to Fernanda Ponderosa that they were finally coming closer to the journey's end. The landscape seemed familiar, although she had never been in the region before. She felt she recognized the gentle hills, rolling in the blue distance into steep mountainous peaks, the clusters of hill towns with walls and houses of creamy-pink stone, the olive groves, the vineyards, and the neat fields of multicolored crops. As the light faded, they approached the walls of the ancient town of Norcia.

CHAPTER FOUR

And so Fernanda Ponderosa was drawing closer to the man who waited for her.

Since he had woken that morning from another feverish night of frenzied dreams, Arcadio Carnabuci had been seized by the grip of an excitement that was bigger than he was. It seemed to squeeze him like an udder. He knew instinctively what was causing it: Fernanda was on her way.

How he got through the day he didn't know. He ran into the midst of his olive grove and tried to bury himself in his work, but he was too fidgety and it was not long before the venerable trees cast him out while they got on with the serious business of nurturing olives.

From there he hurried back to his cottage and danced from room to room trying to straighten things, but in fact making more of a mess. He toyed with the idea of making up the bed with the heavenly sheets, but even he realized he was being premature. The house didn't matter anyway. On this of all days he would be foolish to worry about tidiness.

With a grin smeared across his face like jam, he ran outside and embraced the sky plump and blue with his arms outstretched. He was so happy he began to cry. The joy of anticipation was practically unbearable.

As the day drew on, his elation turned into impatience. As the air cooled, and dusk was preparing to fall over into the plain from the other side of the mountains, Arcadio Carnabuci took up his ax and began to chop firewood to vent his excess energy. He chopped and chopped away with the vigor of a man twice his size. Splintering a great tree trunk, he cleaved it with such force that a little wisp of dust rose up from it like smoke. He was so busy with his chopping that he failed to spot the ramshackle removal truck that limped along the lane at the back of his house and turned into his neighbor's property.

At this point, Ambrogio Bufaletti had reached the frayed ends of his already short string of patience. In his mind he had just resolved to perform an emergency stop and unload Fernanda Ponderosa and her baggage onto the roadside there and then and drive homeward. This journey had gone on too long already. The woman looked well enough, but she wasn't the least bit friendly. There was no chance of anything there by way of a gratuity. As his boot hovered above the foot brake, Fernanda Ponderosa herself spotted a house that she knew immediately was the right one, the journey's end. She cried, "Stop!" which Ambrogio Bufaletti duly did.

The force of the sudden halt shunted the truck's contents to the front, then, just as quickly to the rear. The turtles piled into a tower in their tank, their little legs kicking in the air. The monkey collided with the windshield, sustaining a nasty bruise to his head. In the rear of the truck, Fernanda Ponderosa's belongings combined with one another in a rich furniture stew. In its shock the clock began striking the special tune usually reserved for feasts and holy days. The truck itself shuddered and shed its last remaining accessories: the exhaust pipes, the license plate, and the headlamps. It had run its last race, and this was its death rattle. Signor Bufaletti's mouth issued a string of obscenities.

He began without ceremony to unload the goods in the yard at the back of the house where the truck had been brought to a standstill, and having done so, he hastily drove off before Fernanda Ponderosa could change her mind and ask him to drive on again and try somewhere else.

As the truck coughed away, Fernanda Ponderosa was trying in vain to gain entry into the house. Built of the local pinkish yellow sandstone, it slumped as though hundreds of years ago it had grown into the ground and become a part of it. Even the roof of terra-cotta pantiles was crooked, fitting the shape of the house like a well-worn hat. At the front, the railings of the balcony sagged with age. The shutters, their dark green paint peeling, were all closed like eyelids. Every door around the property was locked.

Darkness was beginning to color the sky gray and the spring air was rapidly losing its warmth. A slight shiver rippled through Fernanda Ponderosa. There was no sound, except for the erratic chiming of the great clock and the far distant sound of someone chopping wood. She put on her cloak and walked around again, testing the doors and trying to peer in through the slats in the shutters. Why had her intuition brought her here? What was this place? What was its connection with her?

Suddenly, a shriek rang out, cutting through the stillness, causing the lonely dove on the roof to flap away in fear. A wild-looking woman had appeared out of nowhere, dropped the milk from the two pails she was carrying over her clogs, and fallen insensible to the ground. She had gone down as though shot. Was she dead?

Fernanda Ponderosa looked around for snipers—there weren't any—and flew across the yard to where the woman lay. No, she wasn't dead; she was still breathing. When she opened her eyes, it was clear she had a pronounced squint, with each eye looking to its side of her head.

"Holy Mother of God!" the woman cried. "The Undead. Silvana, what do you want with me?"

"Silvana?" gasped Fernanda Ponderosa. "Silvana's here? Where?" Suddenly she realized why she had been brought to this place. It was because of Silvana, her twin sister, whom she had not seen in the past eighteen years.

"Up at the cemetery, where else?"

Then, noting the bewildered look on Fernanda Ponderosa's face, the woman added, "She's dead."

"Dead!"

"Yes, she's dead. Been lying up in the cemetery more than

six months. I thought it was her standing there in the yard. Made the hair on the back of my neck stand up on end. Never said she was one of twins . . ."

"Silvana's dead!" Fernanda Ponderosa's voice cracked, and her face was racked with pain.

"She's dead all right," said Maria Calenda bitterly, "struck by lightning. Singed to a crisp. Worst storm in the history of the region. We tried sending a telegram, but couldn't trace her kin. Fidelio is probably dead, too. He just walked away, lost his mind, vanished from face of the earth. They've looked for him everywhere. Savaged by wolves so they say. Business going to ruin. I've everything to do here, all the cheeses to make, pigs to tend, seventeen sows in farrow, goats, cows, sheep. I don't know and what all. Primo trying to do the work of all three of them up at the shop. Sausages. Can't meet his orders. Hams. Spies everywhere. Trouble with the Maddalonis. Pucillo's Pork Factory out to destroy us. Sinister goings-on. The business will be lost. We'll all go to ruin."

Fernanda Ponderosa was stunned. Her sister was dead. She could scarcely breathe. Although they hadn't met in all those years, she always believed that one day they would make up their differences. A shaft of sadness opened within her. Silvana had carried the feud between them to her grave.

As soon as she felt able, Fernanda Ponderosa set out to the cemetery, seeking some kind of reconciliation. It was time to make amends. She left her belongings in the yard where they formed a room without walls or ceiling, inviting the passerby to stretch out on the chaise longue, read a book, pour himself a drink from the refrigerator.

Though the place was unknown to her, she knew where to go without asking. The surrounding hills and mountains did not surprise her. It was as though she were revisiting the area after an absence of many years.

As she walked along in the twilight, her body felt leaden. How could the sense of Silvana's death have escaped her for so long? She, who prided herself on her sixth sense. She reviewed the events of the past six months. Looked back over her dreams, rummaged through her thoughts. Had there been anything that hinted at it, anything at all? She trawled her tired mind but it was blank. She just couldn't explain it.

Without any conscious decision on her part, her legs turned her off the road and through the gates of the cemetery. Instinct led her to the mausoleum, a small villa of rose-colored marble. Inside, a picture of her own face stared out from a round frame, a black-and-white picture she never remembered having taken. Next to it, black letters spelled out her sister's married name, SILVANA CASTORINI, and the dates enclosing her life. She shuddered. She felt like a visitor to her own grave.

Fernanda Ponderosa knelt down on the cold marble and spoke out to her sister, the words she wished she had been able to say to her in life; words that Arcadio Carnabuci, hidden behind the edifice of the Botta family—the nearest he could get while remaining screened—struggled in vain to hear. Although he was too far away to hear the content of her impassioned speech, by craning his neck and straining his ears forward he thought he could detect the cadence of her deep-sounding voice as it rose and fell like a magical fountain. How it thrilled him, like ice sliding down the neck. He basked in the velvet of her voice, and in his nearness to her, and in the tranquillity of the cemetery. He would have been happy to stay like that for the rest of his life.

Although Arcadio Carnabuci had missed the appearance of the removal truck, he had soon been alerted to Fernanda Ponderosa's arrival. Word travels fast in a small place, and the astonishing news that Silvana Castorini's twin sister had come to help out in the midst of the family's crisis was quickly broadcast on the grapevine.

From the description, Arcadio Carnabuci knew, even before he saw her, that the beautiful stranger was his own true love. His Fernanda. She had come at last. He had never doubted it, not even when his situation had seemed hopeless and he knew everyone was laughing at him. And it showed him that the feelings he had had eighteen years ago for her sister, Silvana, were an understandable mistake. Temporarily, before she had married Fidelio Castorini, and, truthfully, for a short while after, he had felt that Silvana had come to the region for him and for him alone. But now he could see that he had simply mistaken one twin for another back then. The right twin had finally arrived. He was beside himself with passion and excitement. He threw down his ax, and went flying out of the yard only to find her already striding along on the way to the cemetery. He followed her there, not having the courage to approach her on the highway.

Although it was practically dark, he studied her. He couldn't make out much, but he loved the sound her feet made on the asphalt. He wanted to lie in the road and kiss the place where she had stepped, but he didn't have time. She was moving fast and it was a struggle to keep up, yet keep enough distance so as not to alarm her. Although he wanted to declare himself immediately, he was grateful for the opportunity to familiarize himself with her in secret.

As he hurried along the road, trailing in her wake, he enjoyed the thought that he was breathing some of the air that she had just exhaled. It had circulated in her perfect lungs, been issued by her adorable lips or nostrils, and had then gone into him. How wonderful. He breathed hard to draw the maximum benefit from this connection between them, though the pressure was about to trigger an attack of the asthma that blighted his life.

CHAPTER FIVE

When Fernanda Ponderosa had said what she wanted
to say, she got up from the ground and stretched out her shapely
legs. Her knees hurt. As she gave them a rub, she suddenly had
the feeling of being watched. Nonsense, she reasoned.

"Scared of ghosts, Fernanda Ponderosa?" she chided herself.

As Fernanda Ponderosa retraced her steps to her sister's
house, Arcadio Carnabuci followed her, and I in turn followed
him. I could not help myself. Where he was, I had to be.

Somehow Arcadio Carnabuci and his love fruit had upset
the delicate balance of nature in the region, and I was one of the
first casualties. Yes, I, Gezabel, the District Health Authority
mule, fell in love with that man. Although he was ridiculous
and puny to human eyes, he was a god to me.

Before last Tuesday I had not been aware of him. I had seen
him, of course, tending to his olive grove, in the fields, and
around the town in the course of my duties, but I had never
noticed him *as a man*. Yet, that night, I was racked by feverish
dreams that left me weak and parched and wobbly on my legs.

His ardent eyes promised me the passion I had never found in one of my own species. The touch of his hand upon my coat was a burning brand. I grew hot and uncomfortable, dewy and soft. We wandered together through the spring grass. We drank from the same crystal brook, by the banks of which he pressed his tiny lips against the soft folds of mine. Later, as we lay in the comfortable bed in his cottage, he kissed my dainty hooves, tickles that sent ripples through my four legs to meet in a fusion of sparks in the long-slumbering layers of my loins. We loved one another through the long, slow hours of that sultry night, and when morning came, I was his, and his alone.

When I awoke, roused cruelly by Concetta Crocetta with my oats, I was exhausted and heavy and bathed in a white foam of perspiration that caused her to check my temperature. I could not do justice to my breakfast because of the butterflies that fluttered in my stomach, thousands of them, tiny ones with the palest yellow wings.

From then on I was struck with a passion bigger than I was. I was a foal again. I began to smell roses in the air everywhere I went. I was jumpy, giddy, excited for no reason; I flushed hot and cold, I trembled, I sweated, I couldn't eat, I couldn't sleep. I lived only to see him and took many a detour past his cottage, which the nurse did not seem to detect, lost as she usually was in her own thoughts, just to catch a glimpse of him that sent my pulse racing and my heart thumping.

My long ears heard music in the wind rustling through the wheat fields. In the sighing of the doves. In the whispers of the night. Above all I loved Arcadio Carnabuci's singing, for his voice could bewitch the leaves on the trees, the rocks on the mountains, the river racing through its course.

When my work for the day was done, and I did not antici-pate a night call, sometimes in the dead of night I came quietly out of my stable and tiptoed to Arcadio Carnabuci's cottage to watch him through the windows. I wasn't peeping, really. I just wanted to see him. I couldn't bear the thought of a day passing without feeding my hungry eyes upon him. Then, the glow of warmth from the candlelight indoors melted my heart, and I would imagine myself tucked up cozily inside with him, just as I was in my dreams.

But outside of my glowing fantasies it was cold. I knew that he did not notice me. Would not even consider me. And this made my despair bitter as lemons. On the outside, yes, I had the appearance of a mule, but inside, couldn't he tell I was a beautiful woman with shapely limbs and glossy brown hair? Yet how could I get Arcadio Carnabuci to notice this, when, even if he looked at me, he saw only the dusty gray fur, now shabby and a little bit moth-eaten, the mealy mouth, the oat-stale breath, the yellowing teeth, and the broad nostrils of a mule? This was my misery. My cross to bear. And now that this glamorous stranger had come amongst us, a real woman, what chance did I stand now?

And so our little procession followed in Fernanda Pon-derosa's footsteps back to the house of the Castorini. He walked in step with her, matching right, left, and right again, trying to feel as close to her as he possibly could. And I did the same with him.

Soon we arrived. The door opened and the house swallowed her up. A little time later a light appeared in one of the upper rooms, the one with the balcony, shining out through the chinks in the shutters. It was a bright night, there was a full moon, a good omen for lovers, and the sky was peppered with thousands of tiny stars, bright worlds millions of miles away, some of which had by this time already ceased to exist. It felt like the most romantic night that had ever been invented.

By the light of the moon and the stars Arcadio Carnabuci noticed a roomful of furniture out in the yard. It seemed strange to leave furniture out, with those thieves the Nellinos down at Folpone, who would take anything that wasn't bolted down and guarded by a vicious dog.

Nevertheless he availed himself of the chaise longue and looked up at the window where his darling remained. He thought happily of how the pink plush had brushed against her bottom as it was now brushing against his. Then, under the influence of the moon and the stars and the singing of the night creatures, the owls and bats and cicadas, the voles and the newts, it came to Arcadio Carnabuci what he should do. He should sing. Sing to Fernanda Ponderosa and thereby announce his love to her in the way he knew best.

Trembling, he could scarcely believe this was happening to him. He knew that here, tonight, history was going to be made. The rest of his life depended upon the song that was about to burst from his lips. The object of a whole lifetime of feverish dreams was here, now, and he wanted to savor the moment, the final bittersweet moment of loneliness and heart-wrenching desire, now so close to being fulfilled, before unleashing the full force of their shared and beautiful destiny. Having waited so long, a minute, maybe two, was in many ways a self-indulgence, but one that Arcadio Carnabuci decided he could allow himself.

With his eyes fixed on the twinkling stars far away in the night sky, he walked toward the front of the house, positioning himself below the balcony with the precision of an opera singer on a stage. Slowly he took a deep breath, then, deliberately, he licked his lips, and from them pored forth the pure notes that ascended to the firmament, causing people throughout the region to sigh and weep at their unbearable beauty. The whole world seemed to have gone suddenly silent, and the sound carried on the slender breezes over immense distances.

Way up on the mountain, the hermit Neddo was roused from contemplation by Arcadio Carnabuci's song, and with a rapturous expression on his face he truly believed he had found enlightenment. Nearby, Neddo's friends, the brown bears, emerged from their caves and began dancing in time to the rhythm of the music that was falling from the stars. Lower down in the foothills, the shepherds stood in amazement amidst the flocks and the newborn lambs and wondered if the beautiful song heralded the Second Coming, and in vain they looked to the east for a star to guide them. Prowling in a circle at the edge of the flocks were the wolves, slavering at the sight of so many tender lambkins, yet so struck were they by the beauty of the song that they abandoned all thoughts of dinner and they, too, raised their voices to the skies.

Closer to home, the citizens of the town threw open their windows or came to their doors enraptured by the sound. Even the baker, Luigi Bordino, broke off from kneading his dough, dusted the flour from his hands, and came to the door of his bakery. Fedra Brini stopped knitting. Speranza Patti stopped reading. My mistress was distracted from her fantasies about Dr. Amilcare Croce.

What could be the meaning of the angel's voice filling the air?

The widow Maddaloni chose to interpret it as a requiem for her husband, who had died in mysterious circumstances earlier in the week.

"Clearly that angel is lost on earth," said Teresa Marta, whose blindness had endowed her with the best hearing in the region. "Can't you tell that from the plaintive beauty of the song? We must help it to find its choir."

But although an extensive search was carried out, the lonely angel could not be found. The baffled citizens stood in the streets with their heads bowed as though in silent prayer, and Padre Arcangelo wandered amongst them uttering benedictions, firmly believing they were all participating in a miracle.

Truly, the only person in the entire region who was not caught up and swept away by the haunting melody was Primo Castorini. Indeed he didn't hear so much as a note of it. He was as usual secreted in the cold room at the Happy Pig working throughout the night to prepare his secret sausage recipes. The concentration while he worked was such that nothing could penetrate his consciousness. All his senses shut down, and he put all of himself—and a lot of him there was—into his sausages. Incredibly, in the past, Primo Castorini had neglected to notice the earthquakes that had rocked the region while he was working, until the roof had fallen down around his ears. So no song, however miraculous, could distract his attention from the serpents of pork that were his life.

Arcadio Carnabuci's song was echoed by the frogs in the lily pads, by the swans on the distant lake, silver in the moonlight, and by the waterfalls cascading in the mountains. It was taken up by the swallows soaring amongst the notes of the melody, and by every humble creature in the region, even the field mice and the naked worms. The almond trees wept a carpet of fragrant blossoms. The statue of the goddess Aphrodite, shoved rudely into the yard by Ambrogio Bufaletti, was silently sobbing, and marble teardrops fell amidst the dust. Just beyond the yard, hidden behind the hazel hedge, I was quivering. My long eyelashes were strung with tears, like crystal beads on an abacus. In them I counted the cost of my hopeless love.

Eventually the shutters were thrown open and Fernanda Ponderosa emerged cautiously onto the balcony. "Who is there?" In her resonant whisper the magic of the night was liquefied.

Arcadio Carnabuci stepped forward into the light thrown

by her lantern but did not cease singing for a second. The song had taken him over, he was its servant, its instrument, and he had no choice but to obey its command.

Fernanda was not exactly as in his dreams. She was a little older than the maiden he was expecting. So much the better. It would be well if at least one of them knew what they were doing. Though more mature, she was much more beautiful than his imagination could render her. The eyes of his heart had drawn her but imperfectly.

Her voluptuous body was dazzling; how much better to sink into her softness like whipped cream, like a goose-down-filled mattress, in place of that slight and angular form he had anticipated. She was bigger than him for sure, but he liked big women. More to cuddle up to. More to keep you warm on a winter's night.

Without missing a beat he absorbed every detail of her like a sponge. Her eyes were not the green of jade; rather they were darkest shade of brown before you reached black. They glittered in the light of the lamp. Her lips were bee-stung and sumptuous. Her hair, despite the frenzied dreams it had caused him, was not the color of tarnished gold. Instead it was black, thick and full, rich, deep, distracting. How he longed to toy with it. It would be a life's work just to adjust it every so often and stop its falling into her eyes or straying across her lips. The fingers holding the lamp were not little slender sticks; they were rounded, bejeweled, lovely. He could write a book about them alone. The poetry of her body would fill a thousand volumes. Of course his pitiful imagination had not been capable of picturing all this.

As she stood there in the lamplight, looking down upon him from the balcony, the bubble of air surrounding them was warm and soft as velvet, although it was only yet the end of April, and the song was filling every spare place in the universe with an unbearable beauty. It was all Arcadio Carnabuci could do to stop himself weeping. But he could weep later. Now he had to sing. Sing now, and then afterward—well, what did the afterward matter? So he sang on, willing her, imploring her, to love him in return. His voice was making love to her, of that there was no doubt. There were contrasting larghetto and allegretto passages, soaring crescendos, followed by the softest diminuendos, which seemed to hang suspended in the air like a feather, during which the enraptured listeners scarcely remembered to breathe.

On the balcony Fernanda Ponderosa waited, shivering slightly although she was not cold. Eventually she stepped forward and opened her full lips. Was she about to join him in song?

"Signor," she said calmly although she was furious, "I beg you to cease singing."

But Arcadio Carnabuci could not stop. It is likely he had not heard her words for his own voice was filling his ears. So he sang on. And while he did so, he kissed the tips of his huge fingers, fingers that were out of proportion with the rest of his meager body, fingers that made Fernanda Ponderosa shudder and indeed did more to harden her heart against him than anything else. Yet Arcadio Carnabuci could not know that his fingers had already nailed down his coffin in Fernanda Ponderosa's heart, and he flicked the offending digits toward the balcony as though scattering his kisses like deep-red rose petals over her.

She responded by retreating inside. Arcadio Carnabuci's heart performed a somersault within his straining breast. Was she coming down to join him, to clasp his fingers in her own jewel-encrusted ones, to declare her own tender love for him? He was weak, about to faint.

Instead she reemerged with a pail of water and upended it on Arcadio Carnabuci. What a tragedy it was that of all the people in the region she alone was unmoved by the song. She had never understood music.

The sudden silence fell like a curtain after a performance that no one wanted to end. Fernanda Ponderosa went back into the room and banged the shutters behind her. Although Arcadio Carnabuci felt the dampness on his head, was temporarily blinded by moisture in his eyes, and became conscious of it permeating his clothing, he was at a loss as to what had happened. This was not the outcome he had anticipated. In due course, an uneasy feeling came to him: that he had somehow offended her. Slowly, and seemingly shrunken to half his former size, Arcadio Carnabuci slunk the short distance to his cottage.

And I followed him through the shadows with my heart about to burst at the unbearable cruelty of the world.

part two

SPROUTING

CHAPTER ONE

Eventually, drained to exhaustion by exaltation and despair, I gave up waiting outside Arcadio Carnabuci's cottage for him to come out and claim me. His every thought was of the stranger. My own situation was ever more hopeless. He would never notice me now.

I dragged my poor little hooves along the road to the town and entered the gate at Concetta Crocetta's premises with more misery in my heart than it was designed to contain. To my surprise and embarrassment, I found the district nurse pacing impatiently back and forth across the yard with a lantern in her hand.

"Where have you been?" she demanded, throwing my saddle over my back. "Maybe I should follow the advice of the District Health Authority and get a moped. Belinda Fondi has gone into labor. We must hurry."

In spite of my exhaustion I allowed myself to be boarded by Concetta Crocetta, clutching her bag of medical implements, and we set off to the Fondi house. With every step I felt I was leaving a little smear of myself behind on the road: broken-heart paste that would be mercilessly kicked over by other passing feet. My mistress continued to chide me for my late-night disappearances and expressed her intention of tethering me inside the stable by means of a rope. But no rope could keep me from my man.

The dark sky seemed scarcely able to support the weight of the swollen moon. The stars twinkled at our passing, and high up in the firmament the faintest echoes of Arcadio Carnabuci's song lingered still.

As we were so late, the labor was in an advanced stage by the time we reached the Fondi farm. No sooner had Concetta Crocetta scrubbed her hands and arms in a basin, donned her crisp white apron, and laid out her instruments than the baby, Serafino, made his entrance into the world. As Concetta Crocetta bathed him, she noted with medical interest the tiny imperfections on his shoulder blades, one on either side. Warts. Or so it seemed.

"Nothing to worry about, my dears," she said to the anxious parents, "lots of babies have them."

But Belinda Fondi could not feel entirely reassured. She wanted her baby to be perfect, and although she was trying hard to be delighted, she wanted to cry.

"It was that singing, wasn't it?" she asked Concetta Crocetta sadly. "That singing's what's made the baby go wrong."

"No, dear," said the nurse, giving her a hug, "superstitious nonsense that. It's warts, plain and simple."

Her work done, Concetta Crocetta left the house and found

me grazing on some embryonic apples in the hedge bordering the yard. While she had been inside, the sky had changed from black to gray. The great butter moon had disappeared over the mountains and the stars were extinguished one by one. The air was warmer, softer. As she coaxed me to abandon my early breakfast, Concetta Crocetta felt something alight on her cap. The same little things began to land on my shaggy gray coat, on the pristine blue serge of the nurse's cape, and on the shiny shoes on her feet. They tickled past Concetta Crocetta's face as they fell to the ground. The nurse caught hold of one and looked at it. It was a feather; the tiniest blue-gray feather, soft as down.

The feathers fell thick and fast. They were raining from the sky. Soon I was covered in them, and I looked around at my back with interest. They were in my eyelashes, in my ears, and in my nostrils, causing me to sneeze. Concetta Crocetta, too, was swathed in them. Her uniform was dappled. Her cap was laden. They were in her hair, her face, her mouth. The ground around us was a snowdrift of down. It was incredible. Neither of us had ever seen anything like it.

At the same moment we both began to laugh. Although we had lived and worked together for twenty years, since the very day she had come to our region, Concetta Crocetta had never heard me laugh before. She was so surprised, and delighted, that it made her laugh all the more, and the more she laughed, the more so did I. We stood there in the humble yard of the Fondis united by the strange phenomenon and by a moment of the most perfect joy.

Still the feathers swirled like dancing snowflakes, and through them, blinking away the ones that had gathered in her eyelashes, Concetta Crocetta saw the approach of Dr. Amilcare Croce. Her heart rippled.

"Amazing!" he shouted while still at a distance, juggling piles of the fluff in his hands. "I've read about it, of course, rains of feathers, but never experienced it for myself."

"Perhaps it's connected with that strange singing in the night. Did you hear it out at Montebufo?"

"Certainly did. Strange thing. Caused uproar." Living practically as a recluse as he did, the doctor had somewhat lost the niceties of conversation, and until he warmed up and got going, he tended to speak in short, spiky sentences, reflectors of his impatient thoughts. "Beasts marching in a line along the hilltops; farmers struggling to turn them back; emergency Masses held in the fields. Superstitious nonsense of course. Must be a perfectly rational explanation for it."

Dr. Croce's voice tailed off; the apple cheeks of Concetta Crocetta had never looked so lovely as they did then, glowing with joy and laughter and health in the rising light. Amilcare Croce, with a glimmer in his eyes, and feathers in his salt-and-pepper hair, seemed transformed into the medical student he once was, as captured in the faded photograph that had pride of place on his desk.

I had stopped laughing now, and looking at the doctor out of the sides of my eyes, I moved away, the clopping of my hooves muffled by the carpet of fluff. At my delicacy the doctor and the nurse felt suddenly embarrassed and looked for the world like two gawky teenagers.

"Everything all right?" He nodded toward the house, predictably taking refuge behind medical matters when they were in danger of becoming personal.

"Fine," she answered shortly, aware of the spell being broken, a snapped thread.

"Mind if I take a look?"

"Not at all."

"Bye, then."

"Bye."

And he was gone. Wading though the swathes of feathers that were already beginning to melt into nothingness. Crocetta Concetta clicked open her bag, and taking a vial from within, she carefully gathered up some of the few that remained as a keepsake. As we rode back toward the town, the sun came up, and aside from the contents of the little bottle and the cherished memories of the three of us, no trace of the phenomenon of the feather rain remained.

Tragically, the doctor and the nurse had never been able to hold a conversation without the most terrible awkwardness on either side. And although in theory they had worked together for the past twenty years when both had arrived in the region, quite by chance on the same day, fresh-faced and freshly qualified, the reality was that they were never more than ships that passed in the night.

Dr. Croce lived alone at Montebufo, a distance of some twenty kilometers from our town, and although in the ordinary course of events this would not prove too significant a barrier to the successful execution of his duties, Dr. Croce was a singular man. His refusal to relocate to anywhere more convenient was coupled with another refusal that had the most profound effect on both his personal and professional life.

His distrust of any mode of transport other than his own two legs had led him to reject the services of the horse, pony, or mule, either alone or with any combination of cart, wagon, trap, or buggy. Neither would any other genus of beast do: he scorned the buffalo and the ox. A childhood accident had given him, along with a cracked head, a lifelong phobia of bicycles and scooters. He renounced the motorized vehicle, be it automobile, truck, or tractor. The sled was unpopular with him, as was the boat, not that the terrain of the region would accommodate these in any case. The helicopter was also ruled out, as it was unlikely the doctor would find one acceptable, and even if he did, the cost would be too high.

In short, the doctor was reduced to traveling on foot the length and breadth of the region, and depending upon the distances involved, a house call could take the whole day to perform.

For this reason the citizens had come to rely for their medical services on my able mistress, Concetta Crocetta, and Dr. Croce, who always arrived too late for everything, was regarded as something of an eccentric. If he ever did manage to arrive on time, it was an unexpected bonus.

While the doctor was nearly always late, we were always in the nick of time. The nurse never needed to be called out and somehow managed to appear at the very moment her presence was required most. Foresight seemed to guide her like a torpedo to the eruption of a boil, the appearance of a rash, or the unexpectedly early pangs of childbirth. With her customary good humor and comforting manner she would set broken limbs, treat the gorings of a wild boar, poisonings by fungi, snake bites, aneurysms, scaldings, drownings, heart attacks, fainting fits, jaundice, and apoplexy.

Her work done, she would move on to her next case, just as the doctor arrived at the house of the first patient, sometimes out of breath, depending on the distance he had traveled. All that would be left for him to do was to stick his head around the door, apologize for his late appearance, and through gritted teeth praise the work of his colleague.

The doctor had, it is true, grown increasingly nimble over the years and had acquired the hard, lean body of an athlete from running over the hills. But occasionally a muscle sprain forced him to remain indoors with his injured limb propped up on a pillow, gnashing his teeth in the knowledge that Concetta Crocetta was making herself even more necessary to the populace, and himself less so.

Yet, in spite of everything, it was widely known that the doctor and the nurse were deeply in love with one another.

The doctor's male pride was wounded at being supplanted by the nurse in the affections and service of the patients, and yet while he did not blame her for this, he could not blame himself for it either. He could not move house. He could not take transport. These were the simple facts of the case, and he could not waste energy on those ephemeral fireflies termed "what might have been."

As he ran across the lonely uplands, and through the wooded valleys, splashing through crystal brooks, and traversing the wide and fertile plains, his thoughts were invariably fixed on Concetta Crocetta, and in a sense he felt he was running for her, that she was the prize awaiting him at the finish line. And yet, when he got there and sometimes, but not by any means always, was fortunate enough to see her, and her every feature, despite their familiarity, he discovered anew, he was struck again by her beauty that was maturing with every passing year that she waited for him, and every time he fell in love with her again as at first sight.

If the nurse lingered a little longer than was necessary on departing from the patient's house; if she accepted an unwanted glass of lemonade or an almond biscuit in the kitchen; if, when we were riding the highways and byways of the region, her eyes had taken to scanning the horizon restlessly in search of a figure who sometimes, often, never came; if she allowed me to walk slowly, meanderingly, on the homeward journey rather than trot—did that make her foolish?

These small things they could do. He could accelerate. She could slow down. The law of averages or probabilities decreed that sometimes, yes, they would meet. And then what outwardly imperceptible but seismic flutterings would discompose them. Yet, in spite of this enormous polyp of tenderness that existed inside each, they were never able to cross the gaping chasm that separated their professional relationship from the possibility of one that was personal. The same pattern was always repeated. There was never any likelihood of their deviating from the script. They had been playing the same game of chess for the past twenty years, and the game always ended in stalemate. And because each precious longed-for encounter was invariably so dissatisfying—stilted, awkward, frustrating—before they had even parted from one another, each was already yearning for the next opportunity when they would meet, and perhaps then things would be different.

The time of the rain of feathers was a defining moment. The conversation they had then was one of their most personal ever, and one that the nurse would always cherish as such along with her vial of down. Concetta Crocetta, an eminently sensible woman, had years ago given up hope of them being anything other than what they were to one another. Too many of her best years had been spent sighing over the doctor. She loved him yes, but she expected nothing.

CHAPTER TWO

Meanwhile, Arcadio Carnabuci was stinging from the hole that had been rent in his dreams by Fernanda Ponderosa's bucket of water. In his mind he went over the scene a hundred times. What had he done wrong? He couldn't understand it. He took the precaution of cursing himself although he was still baffled as to his crime. How could it have turned out so badly? Had he not sung well enough? He considered it the performance of his life. But perhaps he was wrong. He no longer knew what to think. He tossed and turned a million times. His pajamas twisted into a straitjacket.

And yet, he still had hope. After all, she had come. She was here. Just next door. The river of true love never did flow smoothly he remembered his mother saying, and the elder Carnabuci's courtship had, from all accounts, not been a textbook case. He had to take heart. He would make things right. In the morning he would approach her again. It was too late now. By morning she'd see that she had acted hastily.

Later this would be something they would joke about with

their fine family of sons. Yes, it was a temporary blip. She was tired after her journey. She was, after all, grief-stricken over the sudden shock of her sister's death. Perhaps only his timing had been at fault. He had surprised her. And he took consolation from this and resolved as soon as it was light to try again.

A short distance away, Fernanda Ponderosa had found the long-abandoned bedroom and slumped down wearily on the bed. Her own furniture would have to remain outside—she couldn't bring it in now, and perhaps tomorrow she would be moving on again. There seemed little reason for her to stay.

She knew she wouldn't be able to sleep, and that the night ahead would be long. Silvana was dead. Still she couldn't really believe it. Although their rivalry stretched back to the time before they were even born, when each fetus had struggled for her own space, her own survival, there was a bond holding them together, and that neither could sever.

In her tired mind, scenes from the past relived themselves vividly—birthday parties, bike rides, ball games, incidents so trivial she couldn't think why they occurred to her now, why she had even remembered them—and these combined with replayed episodes from the day's diabolical journey, echoes of the lunatic's singing outside, and the looming shadows in the bleak bedroom that formed sinister apparitions.

Fernanda Ponderosa experienced a strange sensation that she was no longer alone in the room and reached for the light switch to dispel her fears. In the sudden glare she found Silvana sitting right at the foot of the bed, watching her. Fernanda Ponderosa screamed.

"So you finally showed up here," Silvana hissed. "Why?"

"I had a feeling, I . . . ," Fernanda Ponderosa stammered.

"Still trusting your crazy feelings, huh?" Silvana interrupted. "Still drifting? Some things never change. So what do you want?"

"Only to put things right between us—is that so bad?" Fernanda Ponderosa's heart was thudding. "I was up at the cemetery just now, trying to talk to you, to explain. Didn't you hear me?"

"I don't spend much time up there myself; the place gives me the creeps. Anyway, save me your explanations. Some things can never be put right. Just because I'm dead doesn't mean you can think everything's fine now."

And with that she vanished, leaving nothing but a hollow in the counterpane where she had been sitting.

"Come on, can't we try?" Fernanda Ponderosa called out, although the room was empty, and she was talking to herself.

"Silvana?

"Where are you?

"Can you come back?

"Can't we just talk?"

But Silvana had had the last word, as she always did, and was gone.

CHAPTER THREE

For the rest of the night, Fernanda Ponderosa was jittery and watchful. Would Silvana come back? It took a long time for her heart to regain its normal rhythm, for her breathing to slow. Again and again, she spoke out to her sister, going over the things she had wanted to say but hadn't got the chance. She was met only with silence, stillness. Every sound in the creaky old house, and the countryside beyond, made her start up in anticipation.

Eventually, though, toward dawn, sleep stole up on her, but it wasn't the restful sleep she so desperately needed. She was beset by horrible dreams. She was being beaten by someone she couldn't see and so was unable to defend herself. She was fighting through layers of sleep to tear herself awake but couldn't reach the surface. She was trying to flee but an overpowering force was holding her back.

She finally awoke and felt a surge of relief that these were only dreams. But what about Silvana—was she a dream, too? Or had Fernanda Ponderosa really seen the ghost of her sister in the night?

As she lay thinking, she became conscious of a voice inside her urging her to stay, at least for a while, and she always listened to such voices. A free spirit, she went where her visions drove her, submitting to the will of the time and tides, and the breezes that sent her in new directions.

Although she was fanciful, Fernanda Ponderosa was also practical. She reasoned that since she had come all this way, she had to try to make peace with Silvana. If she didn't, she knew she would continue to be haunted by regrets. Fernanda Ponderosa also knew that the family business could use her help. In her travels she had gained experience of all kinds of occupations, and working in a pork butcher's would be easier than many things she had done. She hoped this would please Silvana and give her an understanding of her sister's life. Finally, as she didn't feel drawn to anywhere else just yet, she considered this as good a place to be as any other.

So she climbed out of bed, opened the drapes, and threw back the shutters to find the sun was already shining, and from the window she beheld the beauty of the countryside: the plain stretching out ahead of her, its vastness divided neatly into hedge-edged squares containing wheat, rye, and barley. There were rows of sturdy vines leaning on one another's shoulders, fields of young sunflowers nodding their floppy heads, and meadows full of fresh, minty grass.

Beneath the window, the furniture was covered in dew-drops. Already spiders had gone to work spinning glistening strings from piece to piece like Christmas tree lights. A badger had moved into the crib, doves were nesting in the hair of the goddess Aphrodite, around whose plinth were shards of marble the shape of tears.

Fernanda Ponderosa released the family of turtles under the fig tree at the side of the house. The monkey, Oscar, sat up in the branches, watching as she dragged the statue of the goddess into the center of the yard and then hauled the rest inside the house. It was an eclectic collection, and one that jostled for position amongst the dust-covered stuff of her sister and brother-in-law. She didn't take pains with the arrangement. She knew she wouldn't be staying long enough for it to matter.

That done, she set out to find Maria Calenda, who lived in one of the outbuildings on the far side of the property, close to the piggery. Maria Calenda avoided the house as much as possible because she knew it was haunted. Sightings of Perdita Castorini, Primo and Fidelio's long-dead mother, brought her out in monstrous swellings, and she had to plaster herself with a magic emollient before taking to her bed. Other ghosts produced different symptoms, and in the current crisis she just didn't have the time for allergic reactions.

A troupe of miniature goats danced around Fernanda Ponderosa as she crossed the fields. The pigs looked at her dolefully as she passed their pens. Not even the boisterous babies made a sound. Their dolor was because there had been a death in the family.

Fernanda Ponderosa made her way toward the buildings in

the distance. She could detect two or three figures working there. When she got closer, she realized there were only two people, Maria Calenda and a man, and between them, strung up on a frame of timbers and ropes, was the carcass of a pig. Maria Calenda was gathering into a pail the blood poring from a gash in its breast. She had an enormous boil on the end of her nose, which was throbbing like a beacon.

"Ghosts are walking the earth," she announced to Fernanda Ponderosa, gesturing toward her swelling with a hairy finger. "You can depend upon it, the undead are amongst us."

Perhaps she was right.

The man stood up as Fernanda Ponderosa approached. His eyes drank her like a draft of crystal water on a burning day.

He wore no shirt, only coarse waterproof pants and rubber boots, and his great broad, brown breast, which heaved at the sight of her, was smeared with the blood of the pig he had just killed. He was tall. So tall Fernanda Ponderosa had to tilt her head backward to look him full in the face. He was not fat, but built solidly of muscle, and his shoulders were wide. Afterward she could not tell which of his features had struck her first. Was it his hair, a thick and bushy growth of shiny black that had an existence all its own? It was alive. It rippled. It parted and reparted itself. If flexed and shimmied. Or was it his eyes? They were unlike any other eyes she had ever seen. Dark, practically black, like burning coals. They were the eyes of an animal, a wild animal.

Fernanda Ponderosa could feel them physically upon her,

scorching her, but she was used to this. They rested on the puckers of her nut-brown cleavage, on her serpentine curves, on her plump mouth.

"So you're going to save us?" asked Primo Castorini quietly, for evidently it was he, Silvana's brother-in-law. His tone was even, offering respect or sarcasm depending on how you chose to take it. His voice was as deep as his eyes were black.

"Isn't that nice?" he added in the direction of Maria Calenda, who cackled while her squinty eyes flashed between him and Fernanda Ponderosa, enjoying the moment.

Fernanda Ponderosa watched him wipe the sweat from his brow with the back of his hand, leaving a smear of crimson blood there that made him look even more dangerous.

"I'll stay until your brother comes back," she said softly.

He could never have imagined her voice, would never have believed it real. He would always remember the thrill of hearing it for the first time. A bolt of lightning seared through him and down to his crotch. He willed it to stay still.

"My brother isn't coming back," he managed to answer, but barely.

His look dared her to contradict him, but she knew Fidelio would return. Primo Castorini's throat was sun-baked sand. Fernanda Ponderosa felt a splash of hot water against her face as Maria Calenda threw a steaming bucketload over the pig, then started to scrape at its bristles with a hook.

"I'll come this afternoon," she said, "to help out."

"I'll be disappointed if you don't," he said slowly, coming

closer. He was speaking now in little more than a whisper that made Maria Calenda pause in her scraping to extend her ears.

Fernanda Ponderosa turned her back and walked away. The swaying of her hips was the curve of a wave lapping on a beach. A man who had never seen the ocean, he wanted to lie down and drown himself in it. He watched her cross the field until she disappeared from view. When he returned to his work on the carcass, the expression on his face made Maria Calenda cackle again. The stranger would need to watch out.

CHAPTER FOUR

I
t was a beautiful day, the first in May, and already it was unseasonably hot. Summer had come overnight to the region, but nobody could have predicted what the weather had in store for us later on.

In the hedgerows flowers bloomed furiously. The air was overstuffed with their rich perfume and with the sound of insects, fat bees buzzing as they collected their pollen, cicadas singing, busy flies zubbing. Sancio, the daft mule of the Castorini family, was in his meadow, braying loudly. To think that once I had considered allowing him into my heart! The mooing of cows was jubilant, like a church choir. Chickens clucked, goats chattered, and sheep chomped. The earth teemed with life, and up in the blue sky that looked freshly washed, swallows were darting in arcs and circles.

Fernanda Ponderosa arrived in the town, where the streets were full of people discussing the strange phenomenon of the singing the previous night.

Gerberto Nicoletto was demanding compensation from the

Ministry of Agriculture on account of his melons: they had come up overnight, monstrously big, and warped into embarrassing shapes.

Filiberto Carofalo was complaining that his goats had all given green milk.

Amelberga Fidotti claimed her fountain was spouting olive oil.

Earlier in the day a deputation had trudged up the mountain to consult the hermit, Neddo, but no reassurance could be gotten from him: he seemed to have gone into a deep trance and would answer no questions. Although the citizens had waited patiently for him to speak and had held under his nose their choice offerings of meat, eggs, bread, and woolen socks, the savant remained mute, and after several hours of intense scrutiny of the bearded sage, the citizens trudged away again no wiser than when they had come.

After that disappointment they approached Speranza Patti, who was the closest thing the town had to a scholar. She had examined several books in the library and failed to come up with an explanation. This, however, didn't stop her inventing one.

Sebastiano Monfregola had set up a stool and was cutting hair in the street as he did on festivals. When Fernanda Ponderosa squeezed her way past him, he was so struck by her resemblance to her dead sister that he almost cut the ear off Franco Laudato with the blade of the razor.

Fernanda Ponderosa knew the magical sound was nothing but the crazy serenade of the village idiot, but she said nothing.

Before she reached the butcher's shop, she had to elbow her way through the crowd waiting in line outside the world-famous Bordino Bakery. Today it was doing a roaring trade in the carnival atmosphere that had taken over the town. And in addition to the usual breads and pastries, Melchiore Bordino, son of the proprietor, who was a magician with a spun string of sugary caramel, had commemorated the day with marzipan angels whose throats poured forth notes of golden sugar crystals.

Luigi Bordino, Melchiore's father, had inherited the business from his father, Luigi Bordino, who had himself inherited it from his father, Manfredi Bordino, before him. No one could remember a time when there hadn't been a Bordino Bakery in this town.

Bread was Luigi Bordino's life. The smell of bread hung around him in a vapor. At night in bed he thought about bread. The books he read were about bread. The only shows he enjoyed on television were about bread. Bread was his favorite food. He liked nothing better than a hunk of his own bread, unadorned, with no oil, no butter, no cheese or jam. It was good enough for him just as it was.

The Bordino bread was immensely popular. Another bakery was at the other end of the town, and indeed its bread was slightly cheaper than Bordino's, yet it was only patronized by misers. Those who wanted love in their bread joined the line outside Bordino's in the mornings when the smell of heaven hung in the air outside the shop.

But, as the saying goes, a man cannot live by bread alone. Many a long year had passed since Luigi's wife, Gloriana, herself from a baking family in Gubbio, far to the north, had gone to that great oven in the sky. For many years he had harbored hopes of finding a new love, but the object of his affections, my mistress, Concetta Crocetta, never encouraged his advances.

Many times he had kneaded a special dough for her, with love as the secret ingredient. Sweet temptations like fig or pomegranate, raisin and angelica, cherry, or in season, peach, even rose petal. He formed his loving doughs into the most wonderful shapes: wreathes, bouquets of flowers, hearts, fruit shapes, baskets. There seemed no end to his inventiveness. And then with the most tender care he would wrap them in tissue paper, place them in boxes, and deliver them personally to our cottage with a respectfully worded card.

Concetta Crocetta's thank-you notes accumulated under the baker's pillow, but they never gave him the pretext of pressing his suit further. Concetta Crocetta enjoyed the loaves, but the magic ingredient, love, never seemed to rise like dough within her breast, at least not for Luigi Bordino. Though when she ate the bread, she did feel more love for Amilcare Croce.

Luigi shared his home with his son, Melchiore, the pastry cook, and his wife, Susanna. In his heart Luigi could not understand Melchiore's choice. True, it wasn't Susanna's fault that she was stricken with celiac disease and couldn't appreciate the bread that was their life. But Susanna was not an easy girl to get along with. There was something spiky about her. Physically she was the only skinny person in the region. And her tongue was as sharp as her features. She spoke often of progress, about the need to do things in the modern way, and she never tired of singing the benefits of electric ovens to replace the wood fires, and of industrial equipment that would mechanize the kneading process Luigi loved more than anything else. The baker stood firm, but his son, longing for a quiet life, was beginning to support his wife.

The greatest fear Susanna had, and one that often disturbed her sleep at night, was that her father-in-law would remarry, and she regarded with dismay his attentions to Concetta Crocetta. She was not slow to put a curse on the union, and it may have been this that prevented my mistress from responding with more feeling to the baker's suit.

And so lonely Luigi soon began to feel himself outnumbered in his own shop and was fearful of what the future would bring. As a result or perhaps because of his loneliness and fear, he worked harder than ever and made more and even better bread.

CHAPTER FIVE

N ext to the Bordino Bakery stood the Happy Pig, the shop that had been in the Castorini family for generations. Above the frontage, suspended on wires, hung an enormous golden pig that had been smiling broadly for longer than anybody could remember.

Beneath the pig, the window displayed all the fleshy goods to be found inside: ropes of pink sausages hung in swags, ranging from tiny ones the size of olives to whoppers a foot long. There were *ciaccatore, cacciatorini, cotechini, luganige, musetti,* and *mortadelle*. Haunches of cured hams were displayed along with molded cooked hams, sparkling silver trays of sliced meats, sweetbreads, cutlets, tripe, brains, bacon, hearts, livers, and tongue and also whole pigs' heads with apples in their mouths. Squeezed in between the pork products there were jars of lard, mustard, pickled vegetables, and bottles of oils and vinegars.

Fernanda Ponderosa went through the door of the butcher's shop leaving the carnival behind. Inside it was cool and quiet.

The white marble surfaces gleamed, and the air was infused with the pale pink perfume of pork.

In the rear a door led to an inner room. This was the cold room where Primo Castorini worked, preparing the enormous range of fresh and cured meats to feed the region. Everything was made according to the age-old traditions, the recipes for which Primo Castorini held only in his head, and about which he was fiercely secretive. When he saw Fernanda Ponderosa, he felt something inside him being unzipped. In the confined space, his seductive aroma overwhelmed her, and his eyes fixed on hers.

She wrestled her eyes away from his, leaving his hungry, and her glance fell to the counter where she saw his hands among the snakes of sausage. His hands were not what she expected. They were smooth and pink, with fairly long fingers. She felt Primo Castorini had the wrong hands. These weren't a butcher's hands at all. They were the hands of an orchestra conductor or a magician or a priest. The hands were making *cotechini:* stuffing the guts of a pig with a mixture of pork rind, lean pork meat, fat, spices, and boiled pigs' ears. Did she imagine it or did they tremble under her scrutiny?

Primo Castorini felt his usually arid palms breaking into a sweat. Excess moisture would make the meat unmanageable and ruin the sausages. He had to subdue himself, regain control. Already he could feel a straining distorting the line of his apron. He must concentrate on his work. Later he could think about her. Later, when he was away from her, and the fever had cooled, and he could allow himself to luxuriate in every detail of her over and over again. But it wasn't easy. Since that morning, he hadn't been able to get her out of his head. Was it really only that morning, only a couple of hours ago? It couldn't be. In that time she had become his life. His obsession. She was haunting him. She had taken him over. Now she was taking over his business, too. Why hadn't he given her a bigger overall? She was straining out of that one Silvana always wore. He couldn't concentrate with those bosoms peeping in his face. Those dangerous eyes flashing. If he didn't put his heart into the sausages, they would come out bad, and the business, already in jeopardy, would suffer more. There was a chance he could keep it going, but only if he gave it everything. Holy Mother, the smell of her was enough to drive a man out of his wits. With every breath it dealt him a blow to the stomach. He made himself imagine being frozen inside a block of ice. He gritted his teeth. He offered up silent prayers for the stillness of his body.

The air in the room was cool and dry. It was quiet. Almost hermetically sealed. There was no need to say anything. Indeed it would have been unwise to spoil the silence, like breaking open a precious egg. It was a mime or a silent film.

All afternoon they worked together to prepare the secret mixtures, recipes that Primo Castorini knew his rivals at Pucillo's Pork Factory would stop at nothing to obtain. They worked with the precision of surgeons, without speaking, and in truth not needing to speak, for there was almost a synchronicity about their movements, an understanding of what was necessary, which is usually only found in people who have worked together closely for a number of years.

Sometimes, while rolling the pink ribbons of pork on the marble counter, their fingers would inadvertently touch. At such times Primo Castorini flinched as if he had been scorched, and when he did this, the edges of Fernanda Ponderosa's mouth curled upward into a gentle curve that she licked away with the tip of her tongue.

At first, Primo Castorini did not have high hopes of Fernanda Ponderosa's abilities. He considered her the variety of woman who was meant for display. But he was surprised and, although he wouldn't admit it, even impressed. Her large fingers were dexterous, she worked carefully and tirelessly, she was almost as good as he was. He began to feel inferior. She manipulated the meat in a way that made him feel weak. The way she formed the sausages with a rolling motion was an act of poetry. He began to feel the blurriness taking him over again. He drank a glass of cool water and wiped the back of his hand slowly across his mouth.

Despite Primo Castorini's occasional seizures, hot flushes, the palpitations he sought in vain to disguise from Fernanda Ponderosa, they got through an incredible volume of work that silent, smoldering afternoon. Together they made up orders that had been behindhand for weeks. Alone, Primo Castorini could not possibly keep pace with the number of orders that pored in daily from around the world. Yet he would not hire anybody to help him because he trusted nobody with his recipes and was paranoid about spies. In Fernanda Ponderosa his dreams were answered in more ways than one. As she was family, he felt he could trust her with his recipes. But he knew he couldn't trust her with his heart.

Later they were able to move on to processing the hams. These, too, in spite of Primo Castorini's best efforts had been neglected.

For thirty days, each and every day, the thousand new hams had to be rubbed with salt to cure them before hanging them for a year to mature. It was then necessary to rotate the entire stock of hams in the stores to reflect the stage each had now reached in its development. In showing Fernanda Ponderosa how it was done, Primo Castorini massaged his ham like a lover. It was an act of devotion, and one that made Fernanda Ponderosa want to laugh. She could rub salt into a carcass but she couldn't fall in love with it.

Once, running out of salt, Primo Castorini passed behind her to reach for another sack. While he managed to avoid touching her, for her body pulled him like a magnet, the air between them suddenly became alive. It grew momentarily hot and taut despite the tomblike coolness of the room. His body itched, and he couldn't find the right place to scratch.

Finally their work for the day was done. The hams were all salted and put away. The sausages were wrapped in grease-proof paper packets and packed into cartons. The cold room was washed down and gleaming in the light of the fluorescent tube. Primo Castorini could think of no other motive to keep her there. Although he didn't want to release her, he knew that if he didn't get away from her soon, something inside him would burst.

She unfastened the tight uniform and shook out her mane of hair. His eyes never left her. They just couldn't keep away. She was leaving the shop by the front door when she heard his voice breaking the silence. It was soft, only just audible.

"Why didn't Silvana tell us she had a sister?"

"A lot of questions," she replied.

"Only one," he managed. But she had gone, and the darkness outside swallowed her up.

He picked up the discarded overall and buried his face in it. He had no strength left.

As Fernanda Ponderosa walked past the fairy-tale window of the Bordino Bakery, lit up with out-of-season angels and marzipan animals, she did not notice the evil eye of Susanna Bordino fixed upon her. All afternoon, Susanna's mind had been troubled by the stranger who had come among them. The woman was bad news, Susanna could see. Why couldn't people stay in the place they were born? she wondered. She prided herself that she had been born, lived, and would certainly die within the sound of their own bells. Susanna wouldn't admit the stranger was a beauty; there was too much flesh on her bones in Susanna's view. She knew, however, there were some—and amongst this group she numbered her randy father-in-law, Luigi—who might be ensnared by her. Susanna knew his ways.

But the stranger could think again if she thought she was going to snap up Luigi and snatch the bakery from underneath Susanna's nose. Never. Susanna would die first. Of that Fernanda Ponderosa could be sure.

From an upper window, Luigi, too, was watching, his nose clouding the glass, and from that moment on he never gave my mistress another thought. He hurried down to the ovens he had only just closed up for the night and began to knead some dough. Into that dough he put all the passion he had left to unleash. He had never loved Gloriana. It was obvious to him now. The scales had fallen away from his eyes. The first sixty years of his life had been a sham, a total sham. He was now discovering love for the first time, and his heart sang within his withered chest. Looking down from heaven, Gloriana wept; she had given the best years of her life to that man.

CHAPTER SIX

Arcadio Carnabuci was right: Fernanda Ponderosa had come to regret her hasty actions on the previous evening and wanted to apologize for the soaking she had given him.

Blushing like a furnace, Arcadio Carnabuci opened the door to his bedroom and admitted Fernanda Ponderosa, who looked pale, but determined. They had dispensed with the usual chitchat in the parlor. What use had they for words? She had come to him. Nothing else mattered. He watched Fernanda Ponderosa's eyes scan the room. Thank God he had had the foresight to change the sheets. The magnificent new ones made all the difference. He hoped she was impressed.

They looked into one another's eyes. Arcadio Carnabuci was unsure of what he saw there. Was it love? Desire? Laughter? What, for that matter, did she see in his? He felt naked, although he was yet fully clothed. Without drawing her eyes away from his, Fernanda Ponderosa began to undo the buttons of her blouse. Arcadio Carnabuci's mouth went dry. He hadn't had much practice. In truth he hadn't had any practice. Leastways not with other people. He had read manuals of course but it wasn't the same thing. He was seized by a feeling of panic that he didn't know what to do. And what was worse, she would know that he didn't know what to do. And she would hate him for it. Should he make for the door, now that his dream was on the verge of being realized? What would she think of him? Was it worse to repel her by his ineptitude or to make her feel rejected? Already he was on the verge of collapse.

Then something incredible happened. Fernanda Ponderosa, without his being aware of it, had climbed out of her clothes, which now lay in a tender heap on the floor around her feet. She came up close. Closer than anyone had ever come to him before, anyone other than his mother that is, and possibly other family members when he was still a baby, his father, perhaps, possibly his grandmother. So close in fact that he couldn't see her in detail anymore—he lost sight of her—she was just one big sun-browned mass. He realized then he didn't have his glasses on. Where were they? He didn't remember taking them off. But that didn't matter now. Nothing mattered except this moment.

He felt lips on his. Whispering against his. Warm, soft, fleshy lips. He felt the tip of a nose brush ever so lightly against his. The lips were moving around, still in contact with his. They sort of sucked up his bottom lip and manipulated it. He had never experienced anything like this. He didn't know whether it was acceptable to breathe. Whether it was possible even. But then he stopped thinking, and his lips, his whole mouth, responded to the lips of Fernanda Ponderosa. He was kissing. He was actually kissing. And it looked as though he was doing all right.

Without knowing it they had become locked in an embrace. He was standing on tiptoe, trying to stretch himself out as tall as possible. If she was having to stoop, she was hiding it well. Now he was holding her close. Her smell overpowered him. The cascade of her hair rippled over his arms. His bare arms. He was somehow naked. How had that happened? There had been not the least awkwardness or embarrassment. No tangling in the legs of his pants. No shoes that wouldn't come off until their laces had been completely loosened. No smelly socks to be regretted. How had she managed it? How on earth did it matter? He could feel her against him. Around him. Surrounding him with softness. Her arms enclosing him. Her glorious flesh pressing against him. He could feel the gentle pressure of her breasts pushed against him. Her endless legs running up and down the length of his. And all the time their lips working frantically away, trying to make some kind of meaning out of their yearning for one another that was so strong nothing could hold it back. Sucking, plucking, probing. Her hands roved over him. He wished himself bigger so there would be more of him to feel her touching him. Her powerful fingers exerted a pressure on his face, his neck, his chest, his sides, his bottom, his thighs. A smell hung in a cloud around them. It was a smell that was new to him. But it was the most intoxicating smell it was possible to imagine. It was the smell of their two bodies murmuring to one another.

Arcadio Carnabuci began to yowl like the wolf that lived high above in the mountain peaks. He didn't know how he could bear any more of this pleasure, so intense it was agonizing.

Out in the yard, the dog, Max, took up the cry, fearing that the wolves had come down to the plains to carry off the few chickens his master kept. The wretched dog was so insistent. It's barking was so loud.

"Don't stop, I beg you," yelled Arcadio Carnabuci over the din, in a voice that was straining with all the naked force of his pent-up passion. The voice of a man in torment. And a much different voice to the one he usually spoke in.

But Fernanda Ponderosa had stopped. Arcadio Carnabuci couldn't understand it. In that cold, empty place between sleeping and waking, he finally realized he had been tricked by a dream. Max was still barking away. The only spurting was that of Arcadio Carnabuci's tears of rage and frustration.

When he found the light and looked at the clock, he couldn't believe it. Then the awful truth dawned upon him. He had been asleep for more than twenty-four hours. He had slept through the night and through the next day, and now here it was night again. It was the aftereffects of the song that had drained him dry, to the very dregs. He suddenly panicked that he had missed the Maddaloni funeral at which he was due to sing. If he had missed that, he could expect to be attending his own funeral anytime soon. But then he realized the funeral was tomorrow; he hadn't missed it. Thank God. But nevertheless had missed a whole day. He had been robbed of a whole day of being with her. A day he would never recover. What had gone on in that time? He was racked with jealousy. Anything could have happened.

If only he had looked outside and seen me there, waiting for him.

CHAPTER SEVEN

The following day the paths of my mistress and her doctor crossed again. It was an extraordinary stroke of good luck for them, being thrown together twice in two days. The circumstances of this encounter, however, were not auspicious. It was the funeral of the town's undertaker, Don Dino Maddaloni of the Maddaloni Funeral Home. His death had caused a stir, largely because nobody had expected the funeral director himself to die. It was as though his occupation made him exempt. A Rotarian and a player of bridge, he was a big man in the community, and naturally an important man in the local organization of the Mafia.

Concetta Crocetta had been treating him for a stomach ulcer, which periodically gave the undertaker cause for alarm, interrupting the schedule of lavish banquets for which his household was famous. In addition, she had been applying poultices to Don Dino's right foot.

Nevertheless, neither the ulcer nor the gout carried him off. It was a sausage. Or so the rumor told. Word circulated that

Happy Pig sausages, those same sausages made with such care by Primo Castorini, were responsible for bringing Don Dino down in his prime.

Of course there was no truth in this rumor. Don Dino's associates had made it up, for the pork stakes in the region were high, and the Mafia-controlled Pucillo's Pork Factory on the outskirts of the town was out to destroy its rivals. The Happy Pig was the last family concern to remain in business.

The funeral, as might be expected, was perfect in every detail. The widow Maddaloni's grief for the loss of her husband was overshadowed by her regret that he wasn't there to witness his glorious send-off. The six Maddaloni sons, Pomilio, Prisco, Pirro, Malco, Ivano, and Gaddo, were the pallbearers, and they moved with the precision of soldiers on a parade ground. So perfectly timed were their movements they looked like clockwork dolls. No fewer than three priests officiated over the service; indeed, there could not have been more pomp and circumstance if they had been burying the bishop himself.

Whispers that the Maddalonis were reaching above themselves with the excessive and even impious funeral were soon silenced.

In the clouds of incense, the mourners who weren't weeping in their grief were crying because of the inflammation of their eyes and nasal passages. Countless wax candles lit the interior lighter than heaven itself, and the smoke was blackening the ceiling, which had been repainted for the occasion.

In spite of his reluctance and natural shyness, Arcadio

Carnabuci was singled out for the particular honor of singing the Ave Maria, on account of the impression he had made that Palm Sunday on Don Dino. In case his resistance got the better of him at the last moment, he was collected from his cottage in a car, seated between Don Dino's cousins Selmo and Narno. He was even supplied with a robe to wear that gave him the appearance of an overgrown choirboy.

What agonies did Arcadio Carnabuci feel during the service. And it had nothing to do with his grief for the departed. All he could think about was seeing Fernanda Ponderosa again, clearing any misunderstandings, and hopefully delivering a proposal of marriage to her; instead he had to sing at this funeral. Of course he could not refuse. He knew only too well if he tried to assert his will, the ancestral olive grove of the Carnabuci dynasty would be set ablaze. But how bitter were his feelings at the injustice of it all. And how he willed the proceedings to get under way so he could run off as quickly as possible.

In the midst of all of this, through the haze of incense, Dr. Croce spotted the distinctive form of my mistress in a pew a few rows behind him. It was a pure fluke that he had arrived on time. They exchanged nods, and when the service was finally over, after three hours of eulogies interspersed with hymns and readings and the Mass itself, they met in the aisle.

Wearing matching blushes, they both spoke at once in their anxiety to break the ice.

"Lovely service," she.

"Lavish send-off," he.

Their words collided in the thick air and jumbled themselves, causing them both to blurt half-suppressed giggles and then look around furtively for fear that others in the congregation had heard them.

They looked into one another's eyes for what seemed an eternity, but was probably no longer than a few seconds.

"Keep moving there," said someone from behind.

The doctor felt an elbow in his back.

"There's a blockage in the aisle."

"Don't push."

"Be patient, won't you?"

"I can't breathe in this scrum."

"Move along."

The force of the stream pulled them apart. The bodies of the mourners, like a weight of floodwater, came between them. The moment was gone. They kept looking back at one another from their relative places in the surge. Neither could struggle against the current. Were the doctor's sensuous lips forming some word intended for the nurse? She craned her neck to see, but it was too smoky in there, and too dark now that the candles had burned away. Had he said something, anything? He felt her eyes upon him still, brown, warm, smooth. Afterward, when he closed his eyes, he could see them still.

Outside, each was engaged in conversation by interfering busybodies. Policarpo Pinto wanted to talk about his bunions. Filiberto Carofalo wanted a remedy for the aggressive warts that marred his life. Fedra Brini got out her cellulite in full view of the congregation.

In the throng they lost one another, and although the eyes of each continued to search for the other in the swelling mass of people, the figures they sought had vanished.

CHAPTER EIGHT

As soon as Arcadio Carnabuci was able to squeeze through the pressing mass of mourners and discard his chorister's costume, he tore along to the Happy Pig, where he heard with dismay that the object of his dreams was now working. He knew the butcher's ways and he didn't like it at all. Arcadio would ask her to resign at the earliest opportunity.

Fernanda Ponderosa was alone in the shop as Primo Castorini had urgent business to attend to. Earlier, he had received one of his own pigs' heads through the post with a note attached saying, "Don Dino will be avenged." Of course, the butcher knew the dangers of standing up to the Mafia, but he wasn't about to be intimidated. He had gone to Pucillo's Pork Factory for some straight talk on the subject of sausages. His were innocent, and anyone who said otherwise would have trouble on his hands.

As soon as the bells in the venerable campanile had heralded the end of the funeral Mass, Fernanda Ponderosa saw entering the shop the man who had serenaded her the first evening she'd arrived. She knew it was him. She recognized his hands immediately. Large as shovels, clumsy, and totally out of proportion to the rest of his puny body. She looked at the man through narrow eyes. He'd better not start singing now or she'd throw him out on the street. What did he want?

"Signor?" She added a note of steel to her voice for discouragement.

God, she was gorgeous, Arcadio thought. Her uniform had mysteriously disappeared, and she was wearing a tight red dress that clung to her curves and drove him to distraction.

The speech Arcadio Carnabuci had constantly rehearsed in his head since he had woken from his dream the previous night, and in a less specific form over the past twenty years, immediately deserted him.

Now, in the daylight he could see her glory clearly. That night on the balcony, in the shadowy light of the lantern, he had gained only an impression of her, but now he was struck by her startling splendor. Even her teeth were magnificent. Massive. Like those of a horse. He was dealt a physical blow at seeing her in the flesh, the embodiment of his throbbing desires, surrounded by legs of pork and hanging hams.

He felt himself staggering. His legs had gone weak. They seemed unable to support him. Suddenly, it had become unbearably hot. He knew he was growing red. He began to panic. How was he to begin to pour out his heart here in the pork butcher's? There were so many things he needed to say.

He was overwhelmed by the scale, the force of his feelings. He was bursting with sentiment.

Should he reconsider and start to sing? He had always been more eloquent in song than in conversation. The moment was stretching out like elastic. Both were conscious of a rising embarrassment. Fernanda Ponderosa's eyes were sending out arrows and barbs. Why did he not speak?

"Yes?" she said again.

He moved his mouth, but no words could find their way out of the jumble of his brain and onto his lips. To kick-start the process and connect the necessary synapses, he opened and closed his mouth a number of times like a fish.

"Ham," he was able to blurt at last, and his larynx stung with the effort this one word had cost him.

The crisis was over. The tension in the air of the butcher's shop relaxed a little, but not enough to make either feel comfortable.

"Which?" came her curt reply.

Arcadio Carnabuci could only point with one of his huge, purplish fingers at the ham hanging immediately above Fernanda Ponderosa's head. The hand, huge and hairy, hovered in the air right before her eyes. It was hideous. Her disgust could not have been more tangible or more obvious, but Arcadio Carnabuci was blind to it. He had his script and he was sticking to it. In her eyes, full of venom, he could only find love. A fledgling love, he had to admit, but it was there. It had to be.

Fernanda Ponderosa reached up and took the ham down

from its hook. He watched her with fascination. She felt his eyes on her. He broke into a sweat. She flushed. He colored. She wrapped the ham in brown paper and pushed it toward him across the counter.

"Fifty," she said.

He fished a crumpled note out of a pocket and held it out. She looked at it as if it had a disease. She removed it carefully from his grasp with the tip of a finger and thumb, dropped it into the cash register from a height, and slammed the drawer shut. Then she occupied herself behind the counter, arranging jars and pickles, and wiping the already gleaming surfaces with a cloth. Arcadio Carnabuci tried to think of every possibly reason for remaining, but he couldn't and eventually took the hint, and the ham, and muttered, "Good day," and left the shop.

Fernanda Ponderosa did not reply but took a bottle of disinfectant to the part of the counter that had been polluted by the touch of his hands.

He had been inside for twenty-three minutes, and precisely seven words had been exchanged between them. Out in the street, Arcadio Carnabuci was ready to demolish himself.

He hit his head repeatedly against the wall of the Bordino Bakery in full view of the passing crowds.

Policarpo Pinto and Sebastiano Monfregola exchanged glances and shook their heads.

"It's what living alone can do to a man," offered Policarpo sagely.

"He should take a wife," agreed Sebastiano.

"But who would have him?" shouted Luca Carluccio, the wrinkled shoemaker, enjoying the spectacle from his doorway across the street.

"Heard he's been buying bedsheets . . ."

"He's on the edge, that's clear."

Susanna Bordino was not slow in emerging from the bakery to inspect for any damage to the premises she vowed would soon be hers.

"Hey," she barked at my unfortunate olive grower. "Go hit your head on someone else's wall. A block of a head like that thumping against the walls. It's enough to cause an earthquake."

Arcadio, stunned both by his inadequacy and by the blows he had inflicted upon himself, slunk away to his olive grove and confided his bitter secret to his trees. The conversation, such as it was, had not gone well, he knew. When preparing his fine speech, he had fatally failed to take into account his nervousness. He had sabotaged his well-laid plans. How he cursed his self-destructive urges.

I watched him from behind the whispering hedge at the perimeter of the grove, and my eyes were filmy with tears. It shames me to say that my mistress had been obliged to travel to the funeral on foot, for that morning I was once again missing from my stall.

Once Arcadio Carnabuci's tears had run dry and sunk into the compost of the olive grove, tears that would later give an added piquancy to his famous oil, and the soothing air of the ancient grove had calmed him, he began to try to garner together like a magpie the silver slivers of hope from the scrap heap of despair.

In spite of this second setback, he knew she belonged to him, and to him alone. Tomorrow he would spruce himself up—no more half measures—and return to the butcher's shop. There he would declare his love and carry off his prize.

part three

GROWING

CHAPTER ONE

The following morning Arcadio Carnabuci caught sight of his image in the gleaming glass frontage of the Happy Pig and almost failed to recognize himself. He had decided to leave his spectacles at home and could see little without them. Without them his face bore an entirely different character. It looked wrong, and even those who had never seen him before would have been able to tell something was missing from it.

It took a number of seconds for him to identify himself with the dapper be-suited individual with slicked-back hair and red carnation that he saw reflected there.

The suit, it is true, showed it had long been the sole source of nutriment to the family of moths that were resident in his closet, and they watched with alarm as he removed it from the rusty hanger and took it away. "It will be back in time for lunch, my darlings," said the mother to her hungry grubs, trying to sound cheerful, but the prospect of no breakfast was grim.

The length of the pants was no longer as modish as when the suit had been new, now that it had become fashionable for

111

there to be less of an expanse of sock between hem and shoe. But nevertheless, once Arcadio Carnabuci recognized himself, and his surprise had waned, allowing his eyebrows to resume their accustomed position on his face, he felt a surge of pride at the way he had pulled it off.

He fumbled in his pocket for the cue card on which he had noted the most important points; he would not allow his nerves to get the better of him this time. He had agonized over the wording of the card the whole of the previous evening. The packet of one hundred cards he had acquired from the stationer's in the Via Battista for this purpose had quickly formed a crumpled mountain at his feet beneath the table. When he came to the last one, he knew he had to get it right this time. It was now or never. No more mistakes. His hand, feeling a frustration of its own, without any instruction from him, took up the pen, and he could only watch as it spelled out the following words in a childish hand:

"Fernanda Ponderosa, I love you. Be mine."

He scrutinized the hand's words, looking for a hidden meaning. They were simple enough, and to the point. No excess, no wooliness. True, there was none of the extravagant emotion that he would like to have got across, but all things considered, it was good, and taking the independent action of the hand as a favorable omen, he turned out the lamp and went to bed and tried in vain to dream of Fernanda Ponderosa. The gauzy likeness of her hovered somewhere above him, and every time his mind tried to grasp her, she vanished.

The following morning, the flat note of the cowbell once more announced Arcadio Carnabuci's presence in the Happy Pig, and once inside, his weak eyes sought out the statuesque figure of Fernanda Ponderosa.

All he could make out were floating pink masses, which troubled him until he realized they were the hams blurred at the edges by his myopia. A booming voice made him jump guiltily. It was not the voice of Fernanda Ponderosa. No. It was Primo Castorini.

"*Salve,* Arcadio Carnabuci."

Again, the olive grower's mouth performed the motions of a fish. This was not what he had expected.

Primo Castorini was not slow to notice the transformation in Arcadio Carnabuci, and his jealousy reared up like a cobra ready to strike.

"Why, neighbor," he boomed, "your appearance is so changed I hardly recognized you. Has there been another death? Are you on your way to sing at another funeral? What has become of your glasses? Has there been an accident?"

These questions confused Arcadio Carnabuci even more. His eyes kept roving along the shelves piled with jars of pickles that seemed alive, for they were forever changing shape, seeking out the certitude with which he had entered the shop, and the absent form of Fernanda Ponderosa.

"Are you ill? Shall I call Concetta Crocetta?"

Arcadio Carnabuci's fingers felt the cue card in his pocket. But he couldn't turn to that for guidance. At last, after an engulfing silence, just when Primo Castorini's form was moving toward the door to summon help, Arcadio knew he had to get some words out; one word at least. Finally, desperately, like a magician pulling a rabbit from a hat he roared:

"Ham."

It came out far too loud. After the silence that had preceded it. But it was out. It had got him out of a crisis. That one syllable contained all the anguish, all the aching and longing and churning and burning and suffering in the world.

Now it was Primo Castorini's turn to jump. His comfortable frame momentarily lost contact with the ground beneath its feet. He turned around and looked at Arcadio Carnabuci with different eyes. Had he made that sound? A sound unlike any Primo Castorini had ever heard before. Was Arcadio Carnabuci capable of it? Had Primo, and everybody else in the region, misjudged him? Was this pitiful mouse really a man?

Primo Castorini retraced his steps and scrutinized Arcadio Carnabuci, trying to find a trace in this gibbering wreck of some spark of the passion that had led him to release that incredible bellow. There was none. Embarrassed, Arcadio Carnabuci looked down at the flagstones dusted lightly with sawdust and shifted his weight in the shoes that were pinching his toes so painfully. They hadn't been out of their box since his mother's funeral twenty-two years before. They pinched then, and they still pinched now.

"Did you say 'Ham'?" asked Primo Castorini, his incredulity stretched to the limit.

Arcadio Carnabuci nodded feebly.

Primo Castorini lifted one down from the display in the manner one would hold a newborn baby—with love and care and the terror of dropping it—and wrapped it tenderly in waxed paper. It seemed such a waste of such a wonderful ham, to let a fool such as this have it, but such was his business after all. He couldn't allow himself to be sentimental.

"Seems to me you're getting through a lot of ham lately, Arcadio Carnabuci," he said darkly and deliberately. "Fernanda Ponderosa sold you one only yesterday, didn't she?"

At the mention by name of his goddess, his paragon, his muse, his love, his life, Arcadio Carnabuci jolted as though a charge of electricity had surged through him, then struggled to remain on his feet, for how much did he want to lie down where he was and weep.

"You wouldn't want to overdo it now, would you?" Primo Castorini continued quietly, tying the package neatly with a length of string, which he severed with a giant knife. A knife much bigger than was necessary for severing string. The look in his animal eyes as he did so struck fear into the heart of Arcadio Carnabuci. Did it really sound like a threat, or was it only his strung-out nerves, stretched taught as a violin string, that made it seem so?

Arcadio Carnabuci managed to hand over a bill and take hold of the ham, which seemed to weigh so much that he could barely lift it. He shuffled out of the shop a different man to the spry and jaunty one who had come in four minutes previously.

In those four minutes he seemed to have aged forty years. He was broken, and pitiful, in his brilliantine and boutonniere, and in his fine clothes that any other man in the region would have been too ashamed to donate to the *poveri*.

As he left the shop, he was almost mowed down by Fernanda Ponderosa, who had been out running errands. She looked at him as at something she might have stepped in. Before he could apologize for getting under her feet, she disappeared inside and the clanging cowbell was smothered by the closing of the door.

Susanna Bordino, at that moment engaged in a thorough cleaning of her window display prior to a visit by Signor Cocozza of the Environmental Health and Sanitation Department, cast a look at Arcadio Carnabuci that could have scorched the bread then baking in the Bordino ovens. Having done so, she called over her husband, Melchiore, and her father-in-law, Luigi, and the entire line of customers waiting for the bread to emerge hot and crusty and heavenly from the furnaces, then plumping the air with an irresistible aroma, to witness Arcadio Carnabuci's new look for themselves. Instinctively Luigi Bordino knew why Arcadio Carnabuci had dressed himself up like a clown, and jealousy bubbled up like frothing yeast in the normally placid waters of his soul.

Arcadio Carnabuci, even in his confused state, didn't even consider hitting his head on the bakery walls, but looked blankly at the sea of faces in the window, which were themselves watching him. It was only a matter of good luck that the loaves were not burnt black, for Luigi Bordino was as glued to the actions of my poor Arcadio as were all the others.

The impasse lasted until the dazzling May sky cracked open and, despite the heat, blistering drops of rain fell down from a great height, plastering the greasy hair against Arcadio Carnabuci's scalp and causing the moths' lunch to become waterlogged in an instant.

In those moments, which seemed to stretch out and last forever, Arcadio Carnabuci believed that he had somehow died and gone to hell. Still he did not move from the spot, as if he had put down roots there like a tree. Finally, as the rain coursed in rivulets down his face and filled his eyes, making them doubly incapable, he recognized his need for shelter and limped slowly homeward, bowed down by the weight of his ham and his misery.

In the fragrant warmth of the Bordino Bakery, the citizens became animated again, like actors on a stage. Luigi Bordino remembered the bread just in time, and if truth were told, the glazed crust was a slightly darker shade of umber than it would usually have been. Melchiore went back to icing his *pasticcini* with sugar-crusted raindrops, and Susanna loudly denounced Arcadio Carnabuci to anybody who would listen to her.

The cause of the spectacle, Arcadio Carnabuci, had no sooner reached the door of his cottage than the rain stopped with the suddenness of someone turning off a tap. Every rain cloud vanished, the sun burnt fiercely, and within seconds every puddle had dried up. The only reminder of the downpour was the enduring dampness of Arcadio Carnabuci, whose dark front passage became a swamp. To his credit he did not cry.

The waterlogged suit had become as heavy as a suit of armor. The red carnation in the buttonhole had drowned. In the pocket, the cue card had turned to mush, its precious message lost in a splot of ink. Without thinking, he took off the jacket and pants. The smell of must and decay was overwhelmed now by the stench of wet dog coming from the soaking wool. He left it where he had shrugged it off in the hallway. It remained standing by itself. The suit had become his bitter enemy. He identified it now with the terrible morning and blamed it unfairly for his misfortune.

He hauled the ham into his little kitchen, shaded now with failure and disappointment. How different it was from the bright, happy room he had left just a while ago. He put on his spectacles, spectacles he had been too vain to wear, which were lying next to the cup containing the last splash of coffee he had been too impatient to drink. It seemed as though it had been abandoned years before. As he sat down, he saw himself reflected in the kaleidoscope of film on the surface. His haunted eyes looked back at him, full of reproach.

"You fool," read their expression.

Yes. He was a fool. An old fool.

CHAPTER   TWO

In the Happy Pig, Fernanda Ponderosa mopped and pol-
ished, sliced ham, packed sausages, dressed pigs' heads,
stacked shelves, and served customers with a hauteur that dou-
bled her attractiveness. The shop had never been so crowded.
Every man in the region, it seemed, had come in today, and
Primo Castorini knew it wasn't his pork products luring them.

Luigi Bordino had found his muse in Fernanda Ponderosa.
Learning of her fondness for monkeys, he carried in a life-size
bread replica of Oscar. Miniature turtles followed. Fernanda
Ponderosa treated Luigi Bordino like one of her pets and
laughed at his attempts to ingratiate himself. He responded by
scampering about like a puppy.

Others were not laughing. Next door, Susanna Bordino was
foaming at the mouth. Her foolish father-in-law was behaving
like a love-struck teenager, but what could she do about it? The
delicate hairs on Melchiore's ears were soon singed by her com-
plaints. Despite that their fathers, grandfathers, and indeed all
their ancestors had been neighbors, friends even, Primo Cas-

torini had decided to slit Luigi Bordino's throat with the big knife. He would do it, too, if this foolishness continued. Yes, he would stick him like a pig. Let his blood gush out. String him up. Flip out his guts into a pail. Make him into sausages. He knew he would do it soon. Any moment now. God help him, he was going mad.

He brooded the day away. He thought about closing the shop to keep them all out. He couldn't stand other men looking at her. Every lewd glance was an affront to him. So what if the business folded? He didn't care. It wasn't important to him anymore. All he wanted to do was to look at her.

Yes, Fernanda Ponderosa was driving him insane. She had completely possessed him. He looked back on the last forty-eight hours in disbelief. He couldn't even recognize himself. He wasn't Primo Castorini, pork butcher, anymore. He was someone else. But who? He didn't know.

And yet she took no notice of him. None at all. Why was that? He wasn't used to this sort of treatment. He was something of a favorite with women throughout the region. Many had vied for his attentions. His male pride blistered. What was wrong with him that he should be scorned like this and have every other fool preferred to him?

That evening Primo Castorini was entertained by the fragrant widow Filippucci, one of his lady friends, with whom, before this catastrophic change, he had been more than happy to while away a few hours now and again. Yet now he could not tear his mind away from Fernanda Ponderosa.

Even while the widow sang love songs to him and strummed her guitar, even while she was performing for him naked the Dance of the Velvet Doves, even while she assumed the tantric yoga positions she had been practicing for this very purpose, even then he was cursing her for not being Fernanda Ponderosa. How could any woman compete with her? The widow was foolish to even try. He wasn't just bored. He was disgusted.

After he left the widow's boudoir, Primo Castorini pounded the streets. He didn't know where he went or what he did. His boots wore out the sidewalk. Those that watched him were concerned lest he trigger an earthquake, or at least a rockfall. It had taken less than that before now, for the town was built directly above a large fissure in the earth's crust, and in the past even the overenthusiastic cracking of a hard-boiled egg had been sufficient to cause devastation.

Primo Castorini didn't care. Let him cause an earthquake. Let him die. Let them all die rather than he continue to feel this misery. An itching right in the core of him was crucifying him. He held himself stiffly, taut, attempting to control every single one of his muscles, but he could not ease the rubbing, the chafing, the coiling and uncoiling, the contracting, the throbbing, the pain, yes, the outright pain that had sprung a leak within him and gushed like a flood.

My mistress, who just then happened to be passing, gave Primo Castorini a wink and handed him a tube of soothing ointment.

"Rub this in," she said kindly. "It will help."

But Primo Castorini knew no medicine could cure him. Fernanda Ponderosa's face dominated his thoughts. Although she bore a superficial resemblance to Silvana, he could see that they were not similar at all. Silvana was ordinary. Although their features were undeniably the same, some witchcraft had been involved in the formula that made up Fernanda Ponderosa. Her body, her bearing, her strut, were all designed to ruin a man. And how badly he wanted to be ruined.

Why would she not give anything about herself away? He had tried to engage her in conversation. Draw her out. After all, they were practically relatives. Throughout the two torturous, glorious days they had worked closely together, she had revealed nothing. No personal information at all. It was sinister. What was she hiding? What game was she playing? Who was she? What was she? What was her past? What was her future?

Should he go to her now? Throw himself at her feet? Hurl her onto the bed and show her the love of a real man? Only one thing stopped him: he couldn't risk her rejection. He knew he could bear anything except that. That alone would destroy him. Oh, for tomorrow to come so he could be with her again. Feast his eyes upon her. Inhale the overpowering scent of her. Feel the thrill of her body in passing close. How could he endure the slow hours of the intervening night?

His legs took him in spite of himself to his old family home. He just wanted to catch a glimpse of her, that was all. But there wasn't a single light burning. The place seemed deserted. And immediately his jealousy began painting painful pictures for him: Fernanda Ponderosa and a mystery man dining by candlelight at the Ristorante Benito, dancing the tango at Divina, or worse still, lying in one another's arms in a huge circular bed made up with black satin sheets.

But Fernanda Ponderosa wasn't out on the town with another man. Of course not. Romance could not have been further from her thoughts. She was in the ancient kitchen of the Castorini, nursing a cup of cold coffee she had forgotten to drink. It had grown gradually dark as she sat at the long table, remembering the past, trying to draw Silvana into a conversation, but Silvana resolutely refused to appear.

As Primo Castorini stalked off in a bitter rage, he failed to notice the figure of Susanna Bordino, lurking in the shadows, watching and waiting. She, too, had become preoccupied with the stranger, but for a different reason.

CHAPTER THREE

The baby grubs in Arcadio Carnabuci's closet curled up and died for want of sustenance. The mother moth lay in a corner, her wings crushed by the weight of her grief. In vain they had hung on day after day for the return of the suit, but it never came.

In truth, the suit had been consigned to the trash by Concetta Crocetta, who had found it abandoned in the hallway when she had come to call on Arcadio Carnabuci. With her amazing instinct my mistress had divined that something ailed him and had come without being called.

She entered the kitchen to find the figure of my olive grower slumped in his chair wearing nothing but dripping long johns—which he discarded only during the month of August—and an undershirt. I have to say, whatever he wore, I always found him adorable.

What she could not have predicted was the severity of the affliction that seemed to have cut him down so cruelly since the day before. His eyes were open but unseeing, he was unconscious, barely breathing. His flesh was cold and gray, much grayer than usual, and his hair, perching like a pile of tar on his head, gave her a feeling of alarm she had seldom experienced during her long and distinguished career. His whole being indicated the presence of some rare and horrible infection.

Concetta Crocetta took the precaution of donning a pair of rubber gloves, gloves purchased in bulk from one of those very same salesmen who traveled on the *Santa Luigia* in fear of Fernanda Ponderosa, and performed the usual tests. She discovered him to be only half-alive. Perhaps not even that much.

She made him as comfortable as she could, removing the ham that had fallen into his lap, and covering him with a rug from the floor that was strewn with crumpled-up pieces of card. The presence of the ham was of concern to her. She had heard of some bizarre fetishes in her time, but none featured cold meats. Quickly she telephoned for an ambulance.

Through the window I watched anxiously, my nostrils pressed up close against the glass. If only I could have stepped into the cottage myself, I would have saved him: given him mouth-to-mouth resuscitation, cardiac massage, whatever was necessary. I had watched my mistress enough times to be able to perform such procedures myself.

Why did Concetta Crocetta do nothing more? Administer shots of medication? Slap him around the face? Pour cold water on him? Something. Anything. To rouse him from this terrible torpor that so filled me with fear.

In my anxiety I wore away the earth beneath the window with my pacing and left a frost of mucus on the glass that made it increasingly difficult for me to see much of what was going on inside.

After what seemed to me at the time an eternity, but was in truth only a matter of some twenty-seven minutes and eleven seconds, the jangling of bells announced the arrival of the region's antiquated ambulance. The paramedics, Gianluigi Pupini and Irina Biancardi, were saddened by the state of Arcadio Carnabuci, but they were not surprised. Health professionals everywhere had long expected some such calamity to strike him down.

Together they got him onto the stretcher and carried him out. Concetta Crocetta, still wearing the rubber gloves, snared the suit lying in the hallway and struggled to get it into the trash can out in the yard.

I attempted to clamber into the ambulance behind my mistress, but it was clear I was not welcome, and they thrust me outside again, applying their vicious hands to my tender parts and leaving me with bruises. My eyes were full of tears. Was it not natural that I should go with him? I, who loved him best in the whole world? I will never forgive my mistress for her brutality that day. From that time on I carried a piece of grit in my heart toward her that will never go away.

Concetta Crocetta, who was making the journey with the patient, saw fit to apologize on my behalf to the ambulance's crew and with some wadding attempted to wipe up the muck I had left on the floor. She said she didn't know what had come over me. Gianluigi Pupini and Irina Biancardi then struck terror into my already wounded heart by hinting at what they had long known: that the new chief of the District Health Authority was seeking to phase out the use of mules altogether and replace us with mopeds. Standing outside the doors that were just closing upon me, I suffered a double blow. The life of the love of my life hung in the balance, and in addition I was facing dismissal. How could things possibly get any worse?

When they were finally ready for departure, a figure dressed in running shorts and vest scudded into the yard. It was Amilcare Croce, who, now that running had almost become an end in itself for him—he seldom visited patients anymore—was out running when he had got wind of Arcadio Carnabuci's affliction, or perhaps what was more forward in his mind was Concetta Crocetta's presence at the scene.

Whatever his motivation, he made a detour and ran as fast as his powerful legs would carry him in the direction of the Carnabuci olive grove, and the little cottage beside it that bordered the road. He was, as usual, too late. He caught just a fleeting glimpse of Concetta Crocetta within before the door of the ambulance was finally secured, and with Irina Biancardi behind the wheel, it set off for the infirmary in the distant town of Spoleto.

Yet in that fragment of a second, between the closing of the doors, the nurse caught sight of him; their eyes met and Concetta Crocetta knew that he had come there for her. Yes, their eyes enfolded one another in an embrace that became a melting pool of revelation and desire.

Did he only imagine that Concetta Crocetta held out one of her little hands to him? Did she imagine that he held out one of his long, slender hands to her just before that door shut between them so terribly, and Gianluigi Pupini, having carried out the safety checks, jumped into the cab alongside the driver?

As the ambulance trundled over the bumpy yard and turned into the lane, I, of course, followed, for in the midst of the crisis my mistress had forgotten to tether me up. Behind me I could hear the flap of rubber soles as the running shoes of the doctor met the asphalt.

In the lane, our little cortege gained pace, and inside, Concetta Crocetta could see the figure of the doctor as he loped along. How she longed to throw open the double doors at the back and fling herself into his waiting arms, but it wasn't to be.

With her foot on the gas pedal Irina Biancardi eased away as gently as she could, but for all the doctor's training in athletics he could not keep up with the speed of a motor vehicle. And neither could I. Although I trotted along valiantly, I was also soon outpaced and outdistanced.

As the ambulance sped away, its bells jangling, our figures running along the road in its wake grew smaller and smaller until we became just moving dots on the highway, and Concetta Crocetta did something that she had long ago sworn she would never do, and that was shed a tear, for Amilcare Croce, and what might have been.

Arcadio Carnabuci, who lay in a semisomnolent state throughout, was largely forgotten by all the other occupants of the vehicle. But attention would have benefited him little. It breaks my heart to say it, but he was too far gone for anxious looks and the application of a damp washcloth to his clouded brow.

If she had given him a thought, which she didn't, Concetta Crocetta would probably have felt irritated that Arcadio Carnabuci had come between her and the fulfillment of her hopes and dreams. If there hadn't been the urgency to convey him to the infirmary, she would certainly have leapt out of the back of the ambulance, whatever broken bones may have resulted from her actions.

Yet the doctor and I did not give up on our pursuit of the ambulance; we went on, mile after mile. Through Gerberto Nicoletto's fields of mutant melons, through meadows dotted with blue sheep, through olive groves bearing pears. Through herds of mares suckling piglets, through rows of cabbages with human faces turned toward the sun, through vineyards where hazelnuts had replaced grapes on the swinging vines. Everywhere was the evidence of how thoroughly the balance of nature had been disturbed. And still we ran on.

Initially we declined to meet the other's eye; there was between us a small feeling of embarrassment; we had never felt truly comfortable with one another.

Amilcare Croce bore no affection for mules and found Concetta Crocetta wanting in taste for choosing to conduct her business upon me; but this was just one of the many quirks that made her, after all, so lovable.

I, for my part, distrusted the doctor. I could never understand why he had allowed his phobia of transport to mar his life. Why couldn't he get himself a mule for goodness' sake? I had no patience with the way these humans conducted their peculiar romance. They were of the same species, they spoke the same language, they had none of the diabolical obstructions and difficulties that formed a veritable mountain between myself and Arcadio Carnabuci. Why, therefore, could they not speak out, once and for all time, and finally find happiness together before it was too late? If I lived to be two hundred — I was already ninety-seven — I would never understand it.

Yet these thoughts were not uppermost in my mind as I ran along. I was totally dissolved in concern for my beloved Arcadio Carnabuci, not knowing if he would live or die. I ran on despite the pain that was slicing through my lungs like a knife, and the raw abrasions on my horny hooves being grated with every step. I ran on and would continue to run on until I dropped.

Amilcare Croce, however, scarcely knew why he ran after the ambulance mile after mile. He had a sense of urgency, that feeling of if not now, then when? And he could not stop himself. His legs, programmed to run, ran on. With Concetta Crocetta in the ambulance, he wanted to be where that ambulance was. It was that simple and that complicated.

After a while, I took a surreptitious sideways glance at the doctor. It was easy for me as my eyes are set very much in the side of my head already. What did I see? I saw a creature in love, as I was in love, and I saw coiled up inside him all the fear and anxiety and longing and pain and beauty and joy and the frantic, urgent, bursting, unbearable, delicious, tingling, crazy, bubbling, screaming, squealing, laughing, crying, goose-bumping kind of stuff that I had inside me. It was ardor. And the doctor had a severe case of it.

From then on I felt more sympathy for him, and I think he, in turn, was softening toward me. And so, united we ran along, occasionally encouraging the other when the going got harder, the incline got steeper, the breath grew shorter, and like this we covered some five miles with the ambulance still in view, but far in the distance along the long, straight road.

Yet the human or the mule body is only capable of so much. We could not go on thus indefinitely. Inevitably over time we slowed from a robust canter to a trot and thence to a walk. The doctor finally got a stitch in his side and bent over double to relieve it. I walked on a little, hobbling on my painful hooves. The ambulance was no longer in sight. When the doctor stood upright again, I was already some distance ahead of him on the road. I gave him one final glance and went on again in a purposeful way, and the doctor's legs turned him around and headed him for home.

He had a pinking muscle in his calf and his shoulders and neck were grown stiff. Concetta Crocetta inside the ambulance was gone, and he couldn't really go all the way to the infirmary. He did not resent the actions of his legs or seek to reverse their decision. He knew their need of rest, and so, giving me a cheery wave, and wishing me well on my journey, he set off at a slower pace for Montebufo.

CHAPTER FOUR

Inside the ambulance, Arcadio Carnabuci was scarcely breathing. Gianluigi Pupini and Irina Biancardi bantered as usual to try to distract the nurse from her worries, but in truth she was far away, lost in the world of her own thoughts. That sweet, tender Arcadio Carnabuci was left lying there, a lifeless lump. All he could see was the white ceiling of the ambulance and, out of the corner of one eye, the hairs in Concetta Crocetta's nostrils.

The journey to Spoleto was much more speedy for the ambulance than it was for me, and before long it drew up in front of the infirmary, and the emergency team wheeled Arcadio Carnabuci inside. But the battery of tests to which he was subjected could not discover the cause of the malady or determine his chances of, if not recovery, then at least the barest form of survival.

Probes were attached to every part of his beautiful body. He was wired up to a television screen that showed the almost flat line of his heartbeat. His brain function was zero at first, then dipped into the minus, then plummeted clean off the scale.

Soon a crowd of doctors and pimply medical students had gathered around the bed, for nobody had ever seen anything like it. Arcadio Carnabuci was demonstrating signs of being both dead and alive. Technically it should not have been possible, as many of the doctors said, but they couldn't deny the truth of what they were witnessing with their own eyes.

Arcadio Carnabuci, already a miracle to me, had become a riddle to medical science.

Concetta Crocetta, who would, under normal circumstances, be excited by something like this, seemed preoccupied and aloof: she could not get Amilcare Croce out of her mind. He should have been here for this moment. He would have broken into a brilliant soliloquy, expounding his theories amongst these distinguished colleagues. It was not only her love he had thrown away: it was also his illustrious career.

Yet Arcadio Carnabuci, for all the varied opinions of the crowd of eminent clinicians gathered around him, was not dead, technically or otherwise. In fact, inside, he felt as he always did. The problem was that his interior had somehow become detached from his exterior. His mind was fine. But it had lost the ability to communicate with his body.

The faculty of speech had deserted him. His mouth wouldn't issue a sound. Not a snort, a squeak, a hiccup, a groan, or a yodel. Inside he roared, but nobody could hear him. He was trying to tell them that he was alive, that he could hear what was being said. He ranted, at least inside his head, until he had deafened himself. Why couldn't they hear him? What was the matter with them?

Eventually he gave up on his mouth and concentrated all his efforts on moving some other part of his body. He willed his fingers to flicker or his toes, his eyes to blink, his nose to twitch, his willy to unfurl from its nest. Something, anything, so they would stop thinking he was dead. He had had nightmares like this, but now it was really happening. It wasn't a dream.

Inside, he churned and chuffed in vain. Nothing worked. Everything had shut down. He could see the faces peering into his. Hear the many excited voices discussing his prognosis. He could feel the probes in his orifices; they had removed his underwear, so he was completely naked and open to the general view. And female doctors were there as well as male ones. He could see them.

"I've known corpses register more brain activity," said one youthful doctor, tapping the screen with his forefinger in disbelief.

"That's nothing," countered his med-school rival, "I've seen bottled brains give higher readings."

"We have to bear in mind his cerebral activity was at the lower end of the range even when he was well," chipped in Concetta Crocetta.

What was he to do? It was certainly a terrible predicament. He wanted to cry but he couldn't even force tears out of his staring eyes. It was unbearable. If he had been able, he would have killed himself.

Gradually the novelty wore off the way it invariably does, and the cream of the medical fraternity left him alone. The crowd around the bed dwindled until only one or two were left.

Then they, too, drifted away. Concetta Crocetta, who had been quizzed on his medical history and the onset of this strange crisis by everyone from the most elevated professor to the most junior houseman and even by the janitor, was finally released in the early evening.

All of them, from the highest to the lowest, were intrigued by the mention of the ham in the case, and the term *porcofilo* was soon scribbled on his notes. From then on, Arcadio Carnabuci was called this irreverent nickname by the entire staff. Taking one final look at Arcadio Carnabuci and patting him on the arm, Concetta Crocetta set off for home on the bus with all sorts of romantic notions filling her head.

Alone in the ward, Arcadio Carnabuci was left to stew in his own juice. What could have caused this thing to happen to him? He couldn't work it out. He was after all an olive grower, not a doctor. True, he had been overexcited of late. He had suffered several disappointments. Had he suffered an allergic reaction to all the ham he had been forced to purchase recently? Then realization dawned: it was the singing. It was the song that had done it to him. Perhaps his poor, feeble body had that night given more than it was capable of giving. Yes, that one night, that one song, had done it for him. And it hadn't even succeeded in making her love him. Fernanda Ponderosa. In fact he had reason to believe it had made her hate him.

Would he be forced to stay like this for the rest of his life? Had the song cut him off in his prime? Well, if not his prime, then just after it for sure. It was just too awful. To be in the midst of this living death. With everyone thinking he was virtually dead, when inside he was as alive as everybody else. He couldn't bear to think about it. His despair was growing deeper with every thought.

As the bus on which Concetta Crocetta was seated pulled out of the infirmary forecourt, it passed me as I staggered in on legs as unsteady as butter. But the nurse did not see me. Her mind was far away from there. As it grew dark outside and her reflection against the glass grew stronger, Concetta Crocetta lapsed into the sacred secret world of her fantasies, and anybody watching her would have seen a slow smile lighting up her face like a candle. She felt finally that Amilcare Croce and she understood one another. That when they met again, all awkwardness would be over between them. This had been a decisive day.

However, unbeknown to the nurse, the fickle breeze of romance was already beginning to blow in the other direction.

Amilcare Croce was by now at home in Montebufo, resting his sore legs on a cushion and drinking a goblet of the herbal tea that he believed, despite its bitter taste, would hold back from him the gnarled hand of time.

He had thought long and hard on the homeward journey after he had bidden me farewell and watched me follow after my lover to Spoleto. I don't know how he had discovered my secret. Perhaps the expression of my eyes betrayed me, or maybe his own hopeless love had heightened his intuition.

Common sense told him there could be no love between the species. The very idea of a mule and a man finding true love was patently ridiculous. And yet a part of him wished me luck. He thought me a plucky creature and considered me if anything too good for that pitiful wretch on whom I threw my love away at such a great cost to my own well-being.

And what of himself? Was he not also ridiculous? Running along after the ambulance the way he had. It made him embarrassed now to think about it. What had led him to do it? How could he face Concetta Crocetta again? He had made himself look a fool. Hopefully she would overlook it. Never mention it. And he would act as though no guard had slipped from between them the next time they met. For once he thanked the fates that conspired always to keep the two of them apart. With luck, by the time they came together again, she would have forgotten all about it.

I stationed myself outside the window nearest to Arcadio Carnabuci's narrow bed and watched him through the glass. His back was to me, but however hard I watched, forcing my eyes to stay open without blinking, he did not move. Not a single muscle of him twitched. He scarcely seemed even to breathe. I kept my eyes fixed to his chest so long it made me go cross-eyed, but even then I did not see it lift to draw breath. What agonies wrote their words in my mind as I watched him. I willed him to respond to my prayers. Just lift a finger, please, just one finger to show there is still some life left in you. But poor Arcadio could not, and I scarcely felt able to stand under the weight of my misery.

Eventually the supper trolley wheeled its way around the ward and Arcadio Carnabuci remembered he had eaten nothing since breakfast. How good the rabbit stew smelled. He could still detect smells. Even though most of his body had shut down, smells were still able to get in around the edges of the plastic pipes that had unceremoniously been shoved into his nose. Yet there was to be no rabbit stew for Arcadio Carnabuci. He was forced to lie immobile and watch as the other patients, elderly men in pajamas, gathered round a central table to devour it. The supper of the olive grower was administered intravenously by means of another drip in his arm, and it didn't taste of anything except antiseptic.

Arcadio Carnabuci passed the night with his eyes open and unblinking, despite the efforts of Carlotta Bolletta, the night sister on the ward, who tried to close them with her gentle fingers. But repeatedly they sprang open of their own volition. Outside, I kept watch over Arcadio Carnabuci like a guardian angel while he seethed at the injustice of his fate.

While he was lying here, entombed in his own body, he knew he could miss his chance with Fernanda Ponderosa. He hadn't liked the look the butcher had given him the previous morning. He had lost track of time. Concetta Crocetta reported to the doctors he had been slumped in his chair for twenty-four hours. How had she known that? Was it only yesterday? It seemed he had lived a whole lifetime since then.

Yes, he had detected something he didn't like in Primo Castorini then, whenever it was. Doubtless the butcher was in love with her, too. Why shouldn't he be? Fernanda Ponderosa was so voluptuous any man would be a fool not to love her. And he knew the butcher's ways, his shameless pursuit of women throughout the region: teenagers, widows, housewives, mothers, even, it was rumored, nuns. And now he, Arcadio Carnabuci, was making it easy for him to snatch her away, just as his brother had snatched her sister from under his very nose. It was history repeating itself.

Oh, what an unlucky soul he was. But he couldn't allow it to happen. He couldn't allow that wretch of a butcher to steal his bride. Why hadn't she come for him in the first place? He had summoned her up by planting and eating his love seeds, like a genie out of a bottle. He wouldn't accept defeat. He would fight for her. To the death, if necessary.

He just had to get himself out of here. But how?

Again he struggled silently to move his useless body. Concentrated all his efforts on raising just his pinkie, but the slab of sluggish flesh resisted his every attempt to move it. Eventually, exhausted, he fell into a terrible nightmare in which he was lying a prisoner in his own body that wouldn't move.

CHAPTER FIVE

The following morning Pomilio Maddaloni, the eldest of the Maddaloni boys, and the natural heir to his father's wide-ranging business empire, swaggered into the Happy Pig and tossed a copy of *il Corriere* across the counter in the direction of Primo Castorini.

"You're finished, Castorini," he muttered without seeming to move his upper lip, above which blossomed down he was trying to pass off as a mustache.

The headlines screamed up at the butcher, "Ham Leaves Local Man Close to Death." Lurid details followed. There were photographs of Arcadio Carnabuci in his infirmary bed, with seven tubes up his poor swollen nose; in the background you could just see me, peering in through the window. I did not feel the shot did me justice.

There was also a photograph of what purported to be the ham in the case, with the sensational caption "Castorini hams: link with mysterious medical condition," but Primo Castorini could see straightaway it was an impostor. He would recognize one of his own hams anywhere. A new mother was more likely to mistake her baby than was Primo Castorini to mistake one of his hams. But nevertheless he had to admit the ham had a passing resemblance to one of his own, which would be good enough for the uninitiated.

Beneath the article, the rest of the page was taken up with a full-color advertisement for Pucillo's Pork Factory, where the smiling pigs appeared with the slogan "Housewives, can you afford to run the risk? Buy your ham with confidence: come to Pucillo's."

Fernanda Ponderosa, who had come over to look at the newspaper, caused the youth in the too wide pinstripe to experience a sudden surge of hormones that he hadn't felt since puberty. His mouth fell open, and although he quickly shut it up again and made a pretense of being a man of the world, he could not disguise his lust from Fernanda Ponderosa or from Primo Castorini.

Like a pricked balloon he fizzled out of the shop, red and flustered, and burning with a young man's livid blushes. Primo Castorini was stroking the big knife under the counter. He would show that schoolboy. Eyeing up his woman. In his anger he thrust the knife through the offending article into the butcher's block beneath, where it twanged ominously.

Pomilio Maddaloni left behind him a trail of uncomfortable feelings, prickly heat, fury, mirth, moistness, and awkward spaces, which hung in the air until the cowbell rang again, heralding the arrival of Signor Alberto Cocozza of the Environmental Health and Sanitation Department, who wanted to sequester one of the hams to conduct tests upon it.

"It's absurd," said Primo Castorini, boiling with anger. "I can't help what people do with my hams after they leave the shop. I can't be held responsible. It's a conspiracy. They're trying to put me out of business. That's what this is about."

"The Environmental Health and Sanitation Department has a duty to protect the health of the public, Signor Castorini. I'm only doing my job."

Primo Castorini felt he was losing control. He could have believed he was participating in a nightmare, a long, lifelike nightmare. He was physically shrunken, the strain of the past weeks having taken its toll upon him. He was a nervous wreck. Everything was slipping through his grasp. His eyes desperately sought out a meaning in the eyes of Fernanda Ponderosa, but they could find none. She was inscrutable. He trawled there like a deep-sea fisherman but netted nothing.

Did he imagine what happened next or did Fernanda Ponderosa really touch him? As he looked into her eyes like a drowning man, looking for her to save him, did she really come closer toward him, causing the space between them to warp and glow? Then her aroma enclosed him in an embrace, saturating him. She leaned toward him and with her fingertips she touched his, which were spread out on the counter. He flinched at the contact. Her touch burned him and he gasped involuntarily. Her fingers moved up to his bare forearms, thick with solid muscle, and sprouting hairs like a forest. He lurched then, as if in agony. After holding himself so taut and tight for so long, he was about to collapse. He was breathing through his guts, through his willy, quick to rear its head. He almost couldn't bear it.

He wanted to murder the person who made the cow chime chime again and snap the moment off. It was Luigi Bordino, bearing a rose made of bread as a gift for Fernanda Ponderosa, and wanting his first consignment of sausages for the day. He was taking no notice of the note that had come under his door, and that of every other house in the town, advising him to transfer his custom to Pucillo's Pork Factory. He would die for Fernanda Ponderosa. What an honor it would be. The swaggering baker swaggered more at the thought that he was living dangerously.

Primo Castorini smoldered like an underground fire. He had to murder Luigi Bordino soon or he wouldn't be responsible for his actions. Yet behind Luigi were other reckless men all wanting to buy something from her, to have the joy of being served by her or having her personally weigh out their sausages. Slap their pork chops together in the scale pan with the sound of kisses. If her fingers had touched the brains, the great coarse tongues, the rubbery hearts, so much the better would they enjoy them. Some of them were worried by the threats, but they couldn't make themselves stay away.

Though the place bustled with customers, more so than expected after the damaging newspaper article, not a single ham sold all day.

Primo Castorini wanted to close the shop, turn the customers away, fling them out into the street. Sullenly he honed the blade of his knife while Fernanda Ponderosa waited on the customers. Had she really caressed him? His skin was still alive, but bore no traces of her touch upon it. But he couldn't really believe it had happened. He must have imagined it. Nothing about her alluded in any way to a moment of intimacy between them. Nothing at all. She was as arch and haughty as ever and wouldn't even look at him now. He was losing his mind. He felt his reason slipping away like sand in an hourglass.

Of course, the subject of Arcadio Carnabuci was on everybody's lips. Fernanda Ponderosa heard with relief the news that he had been taken away, although she betrayed no hint of this to anyone. Primo Castorini continued to watch her closely. His whole life was now devoted to watching her, it was the one meaning he had left, but he didn't detect any feeling for the olive grower. He had nothing to fear there.

In the town, public opinion was divided. Some people heard the news with relish and were relieved that Arcadio Carnabuci the pervert had been removed from the community. Naturally enough, Susanna Bordino was the ringleader of this group, which included the nuns from the convent, the hairy-faced Gobbi sisters, and Arturo Bassiano, the vendor of lottery tickets, who had inherited a grudge against the Carnabuci clan that stretched back over five hundred years.

But others had changed their attitude to my poor sweetheart and now regarded him as the victim of poisoned pork, rather that the author of his own misfortune.

Primo Castorini's enemies were delighted that his hams had fallen under suspicion, and even those such as the widow Filippucci who had previously championed the butcher's cause were now baying for his blood.

The widow went so far as to join the expedition to visit my darling at the infirmary in Spoleto, a journey of such length that it would have deterred all but the wholehearted. Old Neddo, the hermit, had hired a minibus specially, and it really was a squeeze to get everybody inside. Speranza Patti took the wheel as Neddo had long since lost his license. Next to her sat Fedra Brini, who was busy knitting a balaclava helmet for the patient. Amelberga Fidotti, being small and slender, was allowed to sit on Fedra's lap, but she would keep fidgeting. The rear was occupied by the seven thieving Nellinos and their dog, Fausto. They shoved their way in first and refused to budge. They were joined by Policarpo Pinto with two of his rats, the widow, and three representatives from the town council, who had to contort themselves into the space behind the rear seat.

On the way, Neddo enthralled the travelers with the vision he had seen concerning Arcadio Carnabuci. He had beheld my love riding the golden symbol of the Happy Pig through a flaming sky. While he rode, Arcadio sang mystical songs, songs as old as the earth, if not older, and where he passed, tiny clouds wept drops of olive oil. The listeners were amazed. They agreed the vision was miraculous, but nobody could make any sense of it. They implored Neddo to interpret the meaning for them, but at the crucial moment, as his mouth opened to speak, the sage was struck by one of his characteristic silences, which continued throughout the rest of the journey.

Speranza Patti, who was terrified of the surges of the gas pedal, maintained a speed close to walking pace, and it was some hours before the minibus reached the infirmary. At last, as she witnessed for herself the number of tubes and hoses attached to my beloved's body, the librarian felt a huge wave of compassion washing over her and she realized she had judged him unfairly. While nobody was looking, she slipped into her pocket the only relic she could find: his spectacles. He had no need of them now, she reasoned. From that moment on I considered her my rival, and what anxiety she caused me, I tell you.

All the visitors stared down at Arcadio Carnabuci, pitying him his terrible fate. He could hear all they said, but of course he could not respond. He was a broken man. The relentless struggling of the past forty-eight hours had exhausted him and had taught him the awful truth of his predicament. How he implored Neddo to work one of his miracles, but of course the holy man could not hear him.

Beaten, the spirit of Arcadio Carnabuci retreated to a tiny corner of his brain, where it slumped down with its back against the wall and its tiny hands covering its face in a gesture of despair. Eventually the visitors were forced to leave the ward and they journeyed home, again at a snail's pace. It was a somber group that made its way back to the town, and whereas in the morning they had sung songs to pass the time, on the return journey they were uniformly glum.

Meanwhile, back at the Happy Pig, Primo Castorini was at last able to close up the shop behind the paying customers and draw down the shutters against those who were too scared or too cheap to buy anything, but just wanted to avail themselves of the sight of Fernanda Ponderosa through the great plate-glass window.

His eyes were still glued to her, but she treated him with her customary disdain. As usual when he closed up the shop, she said nothing but left him without a word. After he watched her go, he was mad. He knew then that he had imagined it all. His mind was playing tricks on him. If something didn't happen soon, he would be joining Arcadio Carnabuci in the infirmary. She would ruin them all eventually, he knew. He examined the blade of the big knife for the thousandth time that day, and wincing, he made himself put it away out of sight.

Throughout the weeks since her arrival, Fernanda Ponderosa had kept up her one-sided conversations with her sister, trying to piece together a relationship out of the scraps and tatters of the one they had had in life. But after that first evening, Silvana never came again.

Tonight, however, as Fernanda Ponderosa was reminiscing about a big-eared youth they had fought over as teenagers, but whose name she couldn't remember, she clearly heard Silvana's voice calling up crossly from the cellar:

"Even in death there's no escaping you. Why don't you do us all a favor and disappear off somewhere else? You've caused enough trouble here already."

"Do you have to be so nasty?" Fernanda Ponderosa snapped back, her patience exhausted. She waited, but there was no reply. It was infuriating how Silvana would never discuss anything.

Fernanda Ponderosa realized then that all her efforts had been futile. Silvana was just as unreasonable dead as she was alive. If she didn't want to make amends, Fernanda Ponderosa couldn't do it alone. It was sad, but perhaps she had to accept there wasn't going to be a happy ending for the two of them after all. And so, inevitably, Fernanda Ponderosa began to think about leaving. She always left while she could walk away easily, without a backward glance.

Despite the terrible weight of my sorrow, I knew I could not stay indefinitely at the infirmary, watching out for Arcadio Carnabuci to come back to life. Although it broke my heart to leave him there all alone, I had to return to my duties. I knew that in spite of our long history, Concetta Crocetta needed transport to carry out her work, and if I let her down, she would have no choice but to replace me.

With a heavy heart I relinquished my place at the window and the little spot of turf I had grown very attached to of late, but giving a final loving kiss to the glass, I set off with a sense of purpose. I expected to be racked with pain when I moved, but once I got out on the open road, my muscles eased and I was able to trot along with more vigor than I had known in a long time.

My hooves had healed and were now as supple and strong as they had been in my youth. Feeling good, I increased my pace to a rocking canter, and thence to a flat-out gallop. Love had given wings to my heels. From then on I was able to gallop back and forth between my stable and the infirmary like an athlete.

The more I ran, the more I wanted to run. I understood now what drove Dr. Croce onward. I was no longer exhausted. I was fit and limber. And I ran and ran and ran, feeling the wind in my fur, roaring past my ears, and whistling through my long teeth. Perhaps I was running for my darling as well as myself, since as he was trapped inside his body, I in my running could give him freedom.

CHAPTER SIX

While my angel continued to languish in the infirmary, I determined to perform my duties as well as I ever could. I would give Concetta Crocetta no excuse for acquiring the moped that would see the end of my career. And I have to say we were never busier than we were that summer, even before the temperature soared and we experienced the most extreme heat wave the region had ever known. Not ill health so much as confused health blighted our sturdy citizens, and we were always out on the road making calls.

One particular cause of concern was the Fondi baby, Serafino, delivered during the miraculous rain of feathers. Yes, when Serafino Fondi was born, before the tragedy that so afflicted my loved one, the tiny lumps on his shoulders were a worry only to his mother, who chewed her fingernails over them.

Later, as the nodules protruded farther through his thin baby skin, Belinda Fondi had to resort to subterfuge and disguised them under jackets of her own manufacture, embel-

lished with elaborate epaulets and tinker-bells and baubles sufficient to distract the eye from any suggestion of imperfection.
Passersby cooed over the cherub in the cutesy costumes and
for a time all was well.

But then the bumps developed feathers. At first it was nothing more than a fine fluff. A whisper. A touching peach-skin
fuzz reminiscent of Easter chicks and the warm linings of nests.
Belinda Fondi lied to herself and denied it had come to this, but
soon enough she was forced to confront the truth. As the
mother and child bathed together in the old tin tub, Serafino
laughed and splashed, and Belinda noticed the lumps had
sprouted into wings. Tiny wings, it is true, but wings nonethe-
less, articulated and jointed and clothed in a plumage of pearl
gray feathers that repelled the droplets of water that became
glistening beads on their sleek surface.

Belinda Fondi squinted her eyes and examined the wings.
Tentatively she touched them. It was the strangest feeling.
They were like the wings of a tiny bird. Was her baby turning
into a bird? There was no one she could confide in. People
would say she was mad. They would try to lock her up in the
manicomio, as they did everyone else who didn't fit in. Folk
hereabouts were so old-fashioned, they would be sure to detect
the presence of the devil in the wings, or witchcraft, and then
who knew what might happen as a result? No, she had to keep
it quiet. And pray for the wings to disappear. So Belinda Fondi
took herself more often to the *chiesa* than she had before, and
she prayed a lot harder than she had prayed before. And each

day, several times, and at night, too, she examined the wings with her heart knocking against her ribs. But her eyes could not lie to her. The wings were developing.

Soon Serafino took his first flight. Belinda Fondi was bending to take a cherry cake out of the oven when she felt a rush of air behind her, and when she turned around, the baby had risen up to the ceiling and was flapping his way around the room. Belinda Fondi was not proud of the words that escaped her lips, but her shock was such that she dropped the burning cake onto her foot and hit her head on the table. She called on him to come down, but he flapped on undeterred. Belinda Fondi climbed onto a chair and tried to take hold of him, but the baby had the knack of slipping through her outstretched arms. To her horror she realized the window was open, and she hurried to shut it, fearing he would get out. Later when her husband, Romeo, came in from work, he found the baby still flapping around the ceiling, and Belinda, who had exhausted herself in her efforts to catch him, crying in frustration.

"Don't let him out," she howled as he opened the door, but it was too late, for Serafino was already in the passageway and was making toward the front door. What would have happened if Concetta Crocetta had not appeared at that critical moment and neatly netted the baby in the butterfly net she was carrying made Belinda Fondi's blood run cold every time she thought about it.

Concetta Crocetta had soon made a harness of ribbons and bound Serafino to his crib, and she administered a mild sedative to Belinda Fondi, who could not calm herself, but the nurse herself felt uneasy. She had never in all her years of experience come across a situation like this. She felt bad that she had at the time of the birth dismissed the budding wings as warts, but she could never have predicted this.

When she left the house, she steered me in the direction of Montebufo, for she would not be able to rest until she had discussed the matter with Amilcare Croce, who might have read about the condition in one of his academic journals.

It was around eight when we arrived at the doctor's house. The sun was low, just about to set, and for a while the blue shadows acquired a life of their own. My ears alone appeared the length of a house; my legs were as tall as a skyscraper; and Concetta Crocetta's head with its cap was projected onto the ground as a massive turnip a mile wide.

She had not seen the doctor since the day my Arcadio had been struck down, and that was a while ago now. Although at that time she had felt a cautious optimism, her hope had been extinguished during the following weeks when they had seen nothing of one another. She feared they would be back at the beginning again, and it was with trepidation that she took the lion's-head knocker in her hand and rapped hesitantly.

When Amilcare Croce opened the door, he was rumpled and adorable. His hair was slightly awry. A three-days' growth of stubble was on his chin and cheeks. He was dressed casually in a linen shirt and pants, which had become old friends over the years. His eyes were a little tired. And his smell dealt Concetta Crocetta a blow somewhere deep down inside her, in a place she despaired of his ever discovering. He couldn't have been more surprised at seeing her standing there on his doorstep. She was the person whom, given the choice, he would have most wished to see at that moment. She was also the last person he would have expected. The thin veil of tiredness immediately evaporated from his face, and he ran a worried hand through his hair, regretting he looked a wreck. He wished he had shaved, bathed, changed his shirt, as he had done before many times when false feelings made him imagine she would come. To Concetta Crocetta he looked what he was: the love of her life. She felt a huge surge of tenderness toward him and she had to resist the impulse to seize hold of him and never let him go.

There was a pause, a long pause, as they fought through all the layers of everything they wanted. How they wanted it to be. Joy. Elation. And then finally despair as all the layers of impossibility crowded in and smothered the sparks.

Concetta Crocetta's fears reached her first. After all, she was the one who had made the approach. She had to justify her actions in coming here in this unorthodox way with sane and sensible reasons. Despite her promises to herself on the journey back from the infirmary, every old awkwardness and embarrassment was magnified and strengthened. And the doctor himself flushed scarlet at the thought of how foolish he had been when last they had met. What had started promisingly enough two seconds before had deteriorated dramatically into an abyss of stupidity and shame.

Quelling the quavering in her voice, she explained the strange condition of the Fondi baby. From her rational discourse, no one, least of all the doctor, could have understood the welter of her emotions. The spell was indeed broken. So well did she succeed in being strictly professional that Amilcare Croce was left with the firm belief that she cared nothing for him, and never had, and that all these years he had been laboring under a delusion. His curiosity was roused by the notion of a baby with wings, and he hurried to put on his running shoes and fasten onto his back the knapsack in which he kept the liniment and mustard plasters for his personal use, and also the implements and equipment for his academic care of patients.

We set off together, but despite my recent training I was impeded by the weight of Concetta Crocetta on my back, and besides, I had covered many miles already that day. Although she kicked me mercilessly on my soft, white underbelly, we were soon outstripped by the athletic performance of the doctor. From the first hilltop he waved shyly, then disappeared from view.

The sun, too, chose that moment to sink down behind the mountains, plunging us into an inky darkness that was reflected in the misery of each of us. This had been another day when my beloved had lain like a corpse. How many would follow before this agonizing wait was over?

CHAPTER SEVEN

hile Belinda Fondi lay inanimate as a result of the sleeping draft administered by Concetta Crocetta, Romeo took charge of the baby. But somehow he managed to leave the straps of the harness undone and the window open.

What happened next he was not fully able to articulate, but there came the gentlest impression of the flapping of wings, like a swan simply rearranging its feathers, a breeze as soft as zephyr, and in an instant Serafino was gone. Thrown into sharp relief against the light of the moon, the huge, fat, waxy moon, the baby flapped away, ever higher and higher, trailing behind him a flock of white doves.

At this point Dr. Croce arrived, and he witnessed the tragedy from the yard without being able to do anything about it. He would scarcely have believed it possible, even though he saw it with his own eyes. Romeo Fondi ran out of the house, armed with the butterfly net in which Concetta Crocetta had netted the baby once before that day, and although he ran along, leaping up into the air as far as he could, it was a hopeless cause. Dr. Croce ran alongside the frantic father, and when it became apparent to Romeo Fondi that his son was lost, and that he would have to explain how it had happened to his wife, he collapsed at the roadside and wept.

Together they gazed up into the sky and watched as the baby with wings and the flock of doves grew smaller and smaller, and from being the merest dots in the distance on the surface of the moon, they disappeared into it, and no trace of them was ever seen again.

Dr. Croce let Romeo Fondi weep, and the following spring, where the tears had fallen, sprung up an entirely new and undiscovered species of wildflower that caused great excitement among botanists throughout the world.

When Romeo Fondi had sobbed himself to the brink of exhaustion, Dr. Croce helped him to his feet, and with a kindly arm around his shoulders, he led him slowly back to the house where Belinda Fondi, still immersed in the dreamless sleep of the drugged, was unaware that her baby had been lost to the endless reaches of the universe.

Later, when the doctor had given what little comfort he could to the grieving parents, he left the house and for a while wandered around aimlessly, not knowing which way to go. He could not understand the baby's extraordinary condition, and he was shaken. Medicine, he knew, could not explain it. There was no rational, scientific explanation for what had happened. But he didn't believe in magic. Or in the devil. Or in God. It was easier for him to say what he didn't believe in than what he did. He himself had seen the baby flapping away on wings that sprouted from his shoulders. Never in all his years as a doctor had he read reports of, let alone seen, such things. Where could he begin to seek an explanation?

Amidst the chaos that was the world, there was one certainty. That certainty was Concetta Crocetta. He knew he needed her, and the feelings he had of being out of sorts, disjointed, and not at peace within his own soul or his own body, of being a stranger in a foreign land, all of this he attributed his being unable to get through to her. He was wary of regarding Concetta Crocetta as a general panacea for everything that was wrong in his life, but on the other hand he felt that until this one issue, unresolved for twenty years, and unconsummated, was decided, one way or the other, then he could not look beyond it.

Without realizing it, he had arrived outside our cottage. It came as a surprise to him. He worried he would be seen. But so what if he was? What did it matter now? Only one thing mattered. That he claim her as his own. He walked the block around the cottage a thousand times. If only he could go to her. Hold her. Sink into her and let go of the world, for a while, forever. But his legs wouldn't allow him to turn in at her gate. Each time he hovered there for a second, they moved him on, relentlessly, and continued pounding around the block.

I was not there, of course, for I chose the dead of night for my visits to the infirmary, but when I returned, I detected with my sensitive nose that the doctor had passed much of the night on the block, waiting for his chance with my mistress, as in the past, before the tragedy, I had waited outside the cottage of Arcadio Carnabuci.

Eventually, though, the doctor went away. In the one thousandth and first lap, he realized the hopelessness of it all. Concetta Crocetta hated him. She had been so formal earlier that evening. So brusque and businesslike. He had missed his chance with her, he knew that now. She was punishing him. Years ago, had he spoken, they might have found happiness. But now he knew he was lying to himself if he thought she returned even a droplet of the great ocean of love that he contained for her.

At the same time, Concetta Crocetta was lying awake, gnashing her teeth at how she had messed everything up with the doctor. What a fool she was. A stupid fool. She replayed every word of their stilted conversation. It didn't really qualify as a conversation. More of a business meeting really. Oh, it was hopeless. She was hopeless. She had lost the art of conversation. She no longer knew how to talk to a man. No wonder she was on the shelf. And now because of her stupidity, on the shelf she was destined always to remain.

She was still gnashing away when I turned into my stable, for with my acute hearing I could always tell when she passed a bad night. If only she had got up and gone to the window and looked out, out there, by the light of the great white moon still in the sky, she would have seen Amilcare Croce amongst the roses beneath her window, and then everything would have been so different.

But she didn't. And sadly, slowly, the doctor retraced his steps to his own cottage in Montebufo. It was almost dawn when he reached there, and though he climbed fully clothed into bed, he lay staring up at the one damp spot on the ceiling and couldn't sleep. He was thinking of moving away. Starting afresh someplace else. He had buried himself alive in this depressing hamlet for twenty years. He had stayed on so long because of her. But perhaps it was time to accept the truth, bury it, and move on. He again had the feeling of now or never. If he didn't go soon, it would be too late. It would take time to reestablish himself elsewhere. Perhaps he should return to the city. He was getting too old for these cross-country runs. His bones ached. His whole body hurt. At least in the city his patients would be closer to one another. A brisk walk of an hour, two at most, would take him from one side of the city to the other. He was getting out of touch here. Out of practice. He lacked company, conversation, civilization. He was going rusty like an old nail stuck in a plank of wood. Perhaps going away was the only way to excise Concetta Crocetta from his heart.

ike the doctor, and the nurse, Belinda and Romeo Fondi also passed a sleepless night. Belinda remained at the window, vainly clinging to the butterfly net in case her baby hove into view. She wanted to drown in her own tears. She demanded to know how she was supposed to bear it.

Romeo urged her to come to bed, to take a little rest at least, but Belinda promised herself that she would not rest while her baby was aloft. She would live her life staring out of the windows. She arranged everything in the house so that she could work while keeping watch. She developed the touch of a blind woman, so that she could do anything without having to look at it.

Her eyes were kept solely for their vigil in looking for Serafino in the sky. She became an expert on foretelling the weather. She feared the chill winds blowing from the Alps far to the north. The thought of her baby's naked body shivering and goose-bumped tore her into shreds. And there were the drawers filled with the little warm clothes that she had made with so much love knitted into every stitch. Farmers throughout the region, and others who had reason to watch the weather, came long distances to consult her, and news spread beyond the confines of the region, for unlike the forecasters, she never got it wrong.

Belinda Fondi never interrupted her vigil, not even for sleep, and after three years, Romeo Fondi, who was a patient man, had had enough. After the third anniversary of Serafino's last flight passed with the usual round of outside broadcasts from television and radio stations and a sweep of features in the newspapers, that night he wrestled his wife away from the window and carried her to the bed.

After an initial tussle, Belinda Fondi took the first look at her husband she had taken in three years and fell in love with him all over again. She realized for the first time that she had neglected him.

When, in due course, Belinda was delivered of a baby girl, by Concetta Crocetta, who had eventually been forgiven her role in the tragedy, together the two of them examined her thoroughly, and no trace of any warts were to be found, not even a mole, a blemish, a birthmark, or a freckle. Yet Belinda was not prepared to take any chances, and until Felice was seventeen years old, when she finally rebelled along with her younger brothers, Emilio and Prospero, they were all made to wear harnesses that kept them tethered if not to their mother, then to each other and to the furniture.

part four

HARVESTING

CHAPTER ONE

*Y*et I am getting ahead of myself. Shortly after Serafino Fondi flew away, Primo Castorini's ham was exonerated by the Environmental Health and Sanitation Department. But while the ham was cleared, my beloved remained ill. He lay still, trapped within his corpselike body. Nobody, not even me, knew that inside he was conscious. The staff at the infirmary had grown bored watching for signs of recovery. He was largely forgotten by all except me, Speranza Patti, whose weekly visits were a cause of bitter jealousy to me, and by our priest, Padre Arcangelo, who never failed to say a special prayer for him at Mass.

Often the curtains around his bed were left closed as the other patients found the sight of him depressing. The monitoring equipment, which registered no activity whatsoever, gathered dust. A spider spun its web around Arcadio's toes. A solitary fly developed a taste for his upper lip, and the tickling drove him mad but of course he could do nothing about it. The burden of his own body caused him new and greater miseries with each passing day.

I am proud to say that though he was often in despair, I never once gave up hope for him. I firmly believed that one day he would be restored to life, emerging like a butterfly from its chrysalis. Who knew, maybe in the process he would wake up to me, and we would have a glorious future together? And so I threw myself into my work, and into my nightly runs to the infirmary. I can honestly say that my Arcadio was never out of my thoughts, although I cannot say that I was ever in his.

It grieves me to relate that all the while he lay incapacitated, his mind ran on the subject of Fernanda Ponderosa. Night and day, having nothing else to do, he thought about her. Like me, he was tortured by the peaks and troughs of love. How I cursed my fortune that I was not the source of his anguish. Since the tragedy, most often he was slumped into that corner of his brain furthest from reality, where he took refuge from the despair brought on by his illness. There, tucked away, he ago-nized over whether she would ever love him. Will she? Won't she? Will she? Won't she? Stripping the petals from a daisy.

At times he wound himself up into a frenzy with jealous imaginings on what was happening in his absence, and how Primo Castorini would be taking advantage of his disappear-ance from the scene to ingratiate himself with the future Si-gnora Carnabuci. These were the thoughts that made him feel worse than any other and brought out in him a lather like soap suds that burst stinging his eyes and irritating his nasal pas-sages. Oh, the torture of not being able to sneeze!

Although Primo Castorini was technically cleared of causing my poppet to fall into the coma, nobody bought his ham. The citizens couldn't stomach it. And this, of course, played right into the hands of the Maddalonis and their associates at Pucillo's Pork Factory.

Consequently all the hams that Primo Castorini had so lovingly prepared were left hanging in the stockroom of the Happy Pig. Not just the stockroom either. There was a serious overproduction problem, for the hams take years to reach the required state of perfection, and until the tragedy there could never be enough of them. There were so many hams they had to be stored wherever there was space. They hung in the passage, in the kitchen, in the attic beneath the eaves, even in Primo Castorini's bedroom.

It is true he no longer entertained there as he had done in the days before Fernanda Ponderosa came and removed his taste for any other woman, but still he wouldn't have chosen to share his sleeping accommodation with masses of pork. The hams hung there in neat rows suspended from the beams and watched him. Even while he was asleep, he could feel their dead eyes upon him, rebuking him. An awful lot of money was tied up in them, and this made the situation even worse.

And whether it was because of the weather or because of duress from his enemies, not many people were buying sausages either. People still came into the shop, but they didn't really buy anything, which made Primo Castorini furious. They just came in to gossip.

The weather was beginning to concern everybody. The

intensity of the heat was unnatural. The temperature was rising as if a giant hand were turning up the thermostat. It was a white heat, the very worst kind. The sun was a wound in the sky. The earth baked like a loaf in the searing heat of the Bordino furnaces.

Our lush grass was no longer the color of apples. It was singed brown, and no nutriment was left in it for the poor grazing stock. Naturally crops suffered, too. Tomatoes burst on their vines. Apples, peaches, pears, cherries, and figs fried on their branches. Melons exploded like artillery, and the luckless Gerberto Nicoletto suffered the indignity of a piece of rind puncturing his bottom like shrapnel. My mistress had never witnessed such an injury, and although by means of a delicate operation she was able to extract it, Gerberto Nicoletto never fully recovered his confidence. The incident prompted him to give up the melon farm that had been in his family for fifteen generations, and instead he began a new career as a vacuum cleaner salesman.

Rye, wheat, corn, barley, and lentil crops all blackened. An entire field of tomatoes was subject to spontaneous internal combustion. Everybody feared a forest fire, and those rash enough to continue smoking cigarettes were regarded prematurely as murderers.

The pastures could no longer nourish the animals that depended upon them for their food. The poor sheep in their woolly coats seemed to suffer the most. They just lay on their backs with their legs in the air. There was nothing the shepherds could do. The goats and the cows stopped giving milk and lay in the shade fanning themselves with dock leaves. All the animals dehydrated. Then they shrank up and wrinkled. Maria Calenda spent her days drawing water and bathing her pigs in it. It was impossible to churn butter or curdle cheese.

Dogs went mad and many had to be shot, including Max, my poor Arcadio's dog, which soon started to froth at the mouth. Many, of course, saw this as a sign. Cats started to go mad, too. Then the spiders followed them. They spun curly webs like ringlets of hair. Flies could no longer be bothered to fly and lay where they were, praying for death. Rats, too, lay down, in the roads and in doorways, panting.

One day Fernanda Ponderosa came home from the Happy Pig to discover her monkey, Oscar, had given birth to twins. She found him sitting in the cage nursing the tiny creatures the size of pomegranates. Oscar looked at her with eyes full of reproach that she had not done something about the situation sooner, but in truth Fernanda Ponderosa had suspected nothing. She had not even noticed that the monkey had gained weight, although the sailor suits in which she invariably dressed him were certainly a tighter fit. She called the babies Sole and Luna, Sun and Moon, and regarded their birth as a good omen, although she was surprised she had not foreseen it.

The plump citizens of the town could never remember a summer so hot. People became sluggish and idle and lost their appetites, even for Bordino's bread. Susanna Bordino, the only person in the region without excess weight, was the only one who could remain comfortable, and her boasting made her even more unpopular. But Luigi Bordino was pleased the business was suffering. He was considering selling the bakery. It would fetch a high price and give him more time to pursue Fernanda Ponderosa. What did he care about bread now? As if able to read his thoughts, Susanna Bordino was planning her next move, and had Luigi's eyes not been blinded by love, he would have shuddered to see her evil eye on him.

While most people lay around all day complaining about the heat and the heat and the heat, some enterprising individuals turned the difficult situation to their advantage. Sebastiano Monfregola, the barber, had never been so busy. The heat made everybody's hair grow so fast that many of his clients needed their hair cut every day.

Fedra Brini had taken to making garments out of her cobwebs instead of sails. They were the lightest of clothes, practically weightless as a whisper, as well as fashionable, and she was able to charge a high price for them.

My mistress, of course, who always put her duty first, kept up her punishing schedule of treating the sick and injured throughout the region.

Predictably, heatstroke and rashes kept us remarkably busy. There were a huge variety of rashes from purple spots to green fungus to elaborate curlicues in multicolors that looked like tattoos. There were other strange reactions, too. Amelberga Fidotti grew a beard, her hormones being confused by the heat. Berardo Marta developed a lump on his shoulders that looked like a second head, and many people shunned him, believing this the work of the devil. Those who were overweight suffered palpitations and incredible sweats that made them leave trails in their wake like snails. All my mistress could do was advise them to stay in the shade and drink a lot of water, but soon water supplies were running low.

But even at night there was no relief from the heat. People slept out on their verandas to try to catch the fleeting breeze.

For weeks there had been no rainfall. The rivers dried and shriveled. The lake evaporated, leaving the swans stranded. The mud left by the receding waters turned into dust and blew away. Not even the riverbeds were left. People had dust in their eyes all the time. Belinda Fondi was beset by people demanding to know when it would rain, but she just couldn't tell. There wasn't a single sign of a change in the weather. The sky remained the most blinding blue.

Worse was to come. There were ominous rumblings deep underground. Creaks and groans sounded in the middle of the night, and even during the day. It was obvious to everybody that the earth's crust was thinking of cracking open. It was not going to be a small earthquake either, like those that regularly shook the region.

Holes opened up in roads. Masonry slipped. In the great campanile, the bells became dislodged and clanged incessantly although nobody was ringing them. The mechanisms of clocks were similarly affected, and now nobody could be sure what time it really was.

Susanna Bordino anxiously checked the exterior of the baker's shop several times a day, and each added crack was another crack to her heart. There were landslips and slides. Trees moved.

In my Arcadio's olive grove the trees that had stood in the same place for a thousand years were dancing around, reacting to the pressure beneath their roots. The ghost of Remo Carnabuci, who had loved the grove above everything else, was going crazy. He cursed his unfortunate son, willing him to stop idling in bed and return to the grove. But even if Arcadio got out of bed, there was nothing he could have done.

The cottage where my true love lived fell down in one of the many landslides, so now he was homeless in addition to being unconscious. Such of his meager goods that lay amongst the rubble were picked over by the unscrupulous, who treated it as a rummage sale.

Some people fled the region, gathering their belongings and heading off north or south, east or west, hoping to escape the quake when it came. Even the hermit Neddo abandoned his retreat and set out to return to his wife and twelve children, who lived on the coast near Fano. This was a terrible blow for us, as Neddo had made his home in the mountains for many years and was regarded by the citizens as a sage and a blessing. Predictably he said nothing, and with his knapsack thrown over his shoulder, he walked barefoot out of the shaking district and out of our lives. Although a few followed in Neddo's footsteps, most people chose to remain. This was our home after all, and even if it was destroyed, what would we do somewhere else? Everywhere there was a feeling something was about to burst.

CHAPTER TWO

In the Happy Pig, that sealed world, the writing was on the wall. Primo Castorini had borne the burden of the failing business for too long. Fidelio was never coming back. He had no sons to take over from him. Someday he would have to let it go. Why not now? Let Pucillo's Pork Factory take over. What did he care? For what he could sell the business for, he would buy a yacht and sail away with Fernanda Ponderosa. Away from everybody and everything and be alone with her at last.

Even the pork butcher's succumbed to the heat. Once an oasis of cool and tranquillity, the heat could not be kept out. It permeated through the pantiles of the roof. Through the glass frontage despite its being draped with canvas. It seeped into the masonry, the bricks and mortar; it snaked in beneath the doors. And Primo Castorini was generating heat, too. Yes, he was giving it off. You could fry eggs on his skin. And it wasn't because of the weather. It was because his blood was boiling inside him. Boiling with lust for Fernanda Ponderosa.

In fact, it was hotter inside the butcher's than outside. And of course it wouldn't be much longer before things started to go off. Cured pork keeps better than fresh, but soon the heat would begin to affect the hams stored everywhere throughout the building. Unless the weather began to cool quickly, drastic action would be required. The cold room, though no longer cold, was cooler than anywhere else, and there Primo Castorini shut himself away allowing himself to drift on the raft of his fantasies.

He was still no closer to understanding her. To penetrating her reserve. She treated him always with distance, courteous but cool. Undoubtably he had become addicted to her, but he could never get any inkling of how she felt about him.

Of course, she knew what he couldn't know: that her stay here was coming to an end, and soon now she would be moving on. But before that time could come, she knew that she and the pork butcher would be lovers.

One afternoon she came back from running errands and hurried into the cold room to cool down. Perspiration glistened on her upper lip, and the scent she gave off was like a melon at the peak of its perfection and ripeness, just waiting for you to savor its succulent juices. At least it seemed that way to Primo Castorini.

What had begun that morning in the field watched by the carcass of the slaughtered pig was about to happen at last. All through that long, hot, brooding summer it had been simmering away like a pan on a stove. Now the pan was about to boil over.

Her eyes scorched him like a branding iron. Slowly, deliberately, she walked over to where he stood, leaning against the counter. It was as if she were moving in slow motion toward him. And she didn't stop.

Then she kissed him. In slow motion her lips parted and came toward him, reaching for him, seeking him, and met with his in a fusion that made the earth tremors that had been rocking the district seem like bubbles bursting. Shock waves centered in his groin, they were shooting down his legs and up his back, along his arms; he could feel them running up through his hair, to the tip of each strand, the hair that had a life and a personality of its own, pulsating with the same throbbing sense of urgency that was electrifying his entire body. A mighty dam was crumbling. He gave way to the enormous and overwhelming greed he felt for Fernanda Ponderosa that he had been storing up and breeding since that first time he'd seen her. An insatiable greed.

Now Fernanda Ponderosa's hands were exploring the landscape of his body. It was uncharted territory and she felt herself a mapmaker. His flesh was firm yet pliant to her touch through the strong white canvas of his overalls. She wanted to peel off these coveralls like the skin of an orange and explore what lay beneath. He felt himself being suddenly released from the confines of the canvas. Air was getting in. There was certainly a feeling of relative coolness and ventilation. He was definitely undone.

His hands were full of her, too. He had never felt anything like it. He knew a nanosecond of agony at the realization life was too short for him to feel her body as much as he needed to.

He knew also he had to live out the whole of his life in this moment. The rest of his life seemed suddenly superfluous. Could he die now, like this?

Ghosts of all the sausages that had been produced in this room seemed present with watchful eyes. Every shiny surface of marble, every stainless-steel implement hanging on hooks, reflected their image around the room.

Primo Castorini felt his masculine pride take over. He swept Fernanda Ponderosa up into his arms. She felt weightless, his arms were so strong. She could feel the muscles of the great forearms, which gained their strength from butchering carcasses, holding her aloft.

But then she stopped him with a motion of her hand.

"Not here, not now, not like this," she said between gasps for breath. "Come to me tonight."

As carefully as with an egg he set her down on her feet. She couldn't guess what that gesture cost him. His great chest heaved. He stood back, erect, looking at her in such a way that it was now her turn to lurch. His black eyes bored into hers as though seeking something there he could find in no other place. Did he really have to let her go?

Yes, he did. He had to endure the agony of watching her walk away from him again, but he promised himself it would be for the last time. After that night she would never leave him, ever. He had to make sure of that. He locked the door after her and then let out a roar like a bull in a field.

He tried to compose himself but failed. At last he had her. Or would have her. He could cope with the frustration of the now in the promise of the later. But how to get through the intervening hours? At what time should he go? What did the detail matter? It was four now. He would go at seven. Three hours.

He ran himself a bath. In spite of the heat he needed to submerse himself in water. He let it run deep so that when he got in, the water spilled over the top of the tub and splashed onto the tiled floor. It was hot. But it was good. It eased him. He lay there letting the water into every corner of his body. Steam filled the room with fog. With each small movement more water trickled gently over the edge, cascading like a fountain and hissing onto the floor. Far away in the distance he heard a rumble of thunder.

He didn't allow himself to think what he would do if she refused him later. He just couldn't let that possibility creep in. If it did, it would destroy him. He shut it out of his mind, then locked it to make sure.

He knew he could do it. Knew he had what it takes. He was relieved though he hadn't done it in weeks. So much the better. To have something in reserve. He opened the dungeon where his fear lived, and alongside the threat of rejection he cast down the terror of failure. Then he relocked the door and this time threw away the key.

He stayed in the water until his skin puckered like a prune and he knew then it was time to get out. He shaved, anointed his body with perfume, and dressed in his best clothes and smart shoes. Then he waited for the time to come when he could go to her.

CHAPTER THREE

*O*ver at Montebufo, where even late in the afternoon the plain sizzled like a griddle pan, Amilcare Croce sprawled in the shade of a cherry tree reading. He never changed now out of his running shorts and vest. They were the only clothes that could keep him cool. It was eerily quiet. Even the cicadas were silent. The crispy carcasses of lizards littered the brown grass.

The doctor now spent a lot of time reading learned journals, which were brought irregularly by Carmelo Sorbillo, the postman, who had cut back on deliveries as much as possible, preferring instead to sleep under the counter in the post office.

The heat stopped the doctor from running: he just couldn't do it anymore. Without his running to occupy him he was like a man lost without a map. He tried to keep my mistress, who he hadn't seen in ages, out of his thoughts by filling his head with new and amazing medical theories. But of course he never put any into practice. He lived in theory. He loved in theory. As he lay on his back, looking up at the sky where the angry colors of the sunset indicated that the most terrible storm was brewing, he realized that his life had become nothing more than a theoretical exercise, and this came as an enormous shock to him.

In fact he was immobilized by despair, to think that he had come to this. Once he was so full of promise. When he was a student, before that when he was a schoolboy, everybody had expected such great things from him. He was the one who won the prizes. He was going change the world. His feet would tread the path of glory. And what had happened? How had it all gone so badly wrong? He had done nothing. Nothing. He had abandoned his work. His great career. He hadn't even been capable of loving a woman. He was about to go mad with fury. He had ruined his life. It was a complete mess.

When he emerged from his reverie, he was as fired up as the sky. He got up, threw the periodical into the hedge, left everything as it was, radio playing in the kitchen, door open, and he just walked away from the house. He didn't even stop to put on a pair of shoes.

The road that passed his house burned his feet like hot coals, and his skin stuck to the asphalt with a hissing sound. Cursing, he hopped up and down, then started to run. Taking long, long strides, and bouncing on his toes to reduce the burning. Not even knowing where he was going. He just put one foot ahead of the other. Without thinking. With no plan. Was he just going to run and keep on running? Leave the region with no word to anybody and never come back?

He felt the roasting air burnishing his face. His hair frizzled. And he began to run faster. In spite of the heat, he flew along, faster than he had ever run before. His inner rage burned inside brighter than the angry sun and filled him with an endless supply of energy, which was fueling his long legs with running juice. People who saw him along the way found it remarkable. His nearest neighbor, Giuseppe Mormile, watched him trail past like a blazing comet and himself puffed over to his wife, Immacolata, who was halfheartedly tending to what remained of her lettuce crop.

"Look," he said simply, pointing at the doctor, who was kicking up a trail of burning dust along the road. Above him the sun had turned from red to purple. It was an ominous sign.

Immacolata couldn't understand it. It was as though someone had wound up the clockwork world and set it on a faster speed. She liked things slow. While everything around her accelerated, she bent down to her lettuces, slow as the snail creeping on its leaf. The two retained their slowness in a world that had gone mad.

The doctor ran on. He didn't think where he was going. He just put his trust in his legs. They would take him where he needed to go. He would go with them. He was the slave of his legs. He started to breathe, and the air entered and left his lungs in such a perfect motion that he felt he had never breathed before that moment. It empowered him and gave speed to his legs, urging him onward.

Only when he reached the street where Concetta Crocetta lived did he realize this was his destination. Where his legs had brought him. He was not even short of breath, despite the searing heat. In fact, as he ran, the years had fallen away from him, and he looked twenty-five, not fifty. His skin glowed with youth and health. And now a smile spread over his features as he accepted everything.

Already a crowd had gathered under parasols in the Via Alfieri to celebrate with the doctor and the nurse. Everyone was clapping and laughing. Out of somewhere, and on short notice, the town brass band had assembled in full uniform, and the bandsmen were sweating their way through a medley of popular numbers while a troupe of majorettes twirled their batons.

Dr. Croce, however, saw and heard none of this. For him the world was strangely silent. All he could hear was the pulsing of the blood in his ears and the no longer timid voice of his heart calling out the name of Concetta Crocetta.

In her little cottage, my mistress was not aware of the carnival taking place outside. She had just fed me my oats out in the stable, and now back in her kitchen she was demolishing a tub of ice cream. Her hair was pulled up into a straggly bun and she was wearing nothing but her silk slip, and even that was too hot.

The doctor was like one in a dream, although he was wide-awake and fully conscious. His body seemed to be acting without any commands from his brain. Even if he wanted to, which he didn't, he couldn't have called a halt to what his body had begun and was going to follow through with. Stored up within his bones and blood and cells and sinews were the memories or blueprints of all the actions he should have carried out over the past twenty years but didn't.

He opened the back door to the cottage without knocking, as though coming home, and entered the tiny kitchen. Obviously, he had never been inside before. It did not even surprise Concetta Crocetta to see her door opening and the tall person of the doctor stoop slightly to come inside. There was not the slightest embarrassment or hesitation on either side. The careful observer would have noticed Concetta Crocetta replace the spoon she had been raising to her lips in the tub of ice cream and set it down on the table.

For a long moment they looked deep into one another's eyes as they had longed to do for so many years. They seemed to swim there, unhurried, exploring, probing into the hidden depths, the secret corners, and instinctively they understood everything.

It seemed obvious that the doctor should simply admit himself into her home, that she should stop eating ice cream, that she should not feel the slightest amazement. But that moment, the last of the old moments, the cusp of the new and the old joining, could not last forever, and of course nobody should want it to. With one long stride of his athletic legs the doctor crossed the room and was standing before Concetta Crocetta not as a doctor, but as a man.

CHAPTER FOUR

In the kitchen of number 37 Via Alfieri time was standing still as the doctor and the nurse sought to make up for twenty years of starved passions, oblivious to the ominous rumbling of the storm that was gathering in the sky.

The air was electric. The suspense was growing. Everybody waited on tenterhooks. The storm would surely come and bring with it cooler temperatures and much needed rain. Already in their imagination, the citizens were running out naked into the rain and glorying in it, feeling the delicious icy drops tingling on their bodies, dancing, laughing, singing, with no embarrassment at all, just rejoicing at last that the terrible heat was over.

First the thunder started. The foreshadowing echoes of which Primo Castorini heard while languishing in his bathtub. At least it sounded like thunder. Although many were convinced it was the cracking of the earth beneath their feet. Great bellows of thunder set the wolves howling up in the foothills. It echoed around the basin formed by the circling mountains and resounded across the plain, setting up a ripple of thunders that were magnified amid copies and originals; the peals clanged against one another and merged. A frightful din followed. The cows lowed in the meadows, a low, eerie lowing that sent shivers down the spines of those who heard it.

The thunder rumbled on. It went on so long the citizens of the region began to fear that there would just be thunder and nothing else. No storm. No rain. And no end to the heat.

Then, later, much later, when we had nearly given up hope, a flash of lightning cut the sky open and laid it bare. The sky went white and stayed white.

In the blinding white light Primo Castorini left the Happy Pig and set out in the direction of his old family home. There would be no more holding back. He was going to Fernanda Ponderosa, and he was going to have her. He marched along with a determined stride, and those who saw him had no doubt as to where he was going and what he was going to do when he got there.

That same lightning flash that sent Primo Castorini out on his mission was responsible for amazing phenomena. Events that nobody could ever have predicted.

It woke a sleeper. Yes, it roused Fidelio Castorini, who had been in a coma in a cave high up in the mountains for the past nine months since Silvana's death. He opened his eyes and stared about him in the blinding whiteness. His mind was numb. He didn't know where he was or why. He had no recollection of the catastrophe that had led him to wander away. The ground was hard: it was solid stone. He sat up. His body was stiff. Where was he? He didn't recognize anything. But the light showed him the way out of the cave, and cautiously he got to his feet and hobbled out into the night. Outside he became aware of where he was. He was somehow at the top of the highest mountain, and in the whiteness he could see the whole of the great plain below him, stretching out for many miles. His eyes strained toward something in the far distance. Home. He would go home.

The mighty flash awoke a second sleeper. My Arcadio. My own true love. Tears of joy fill my eyes as I think about it. He was alive and restored to me. Yes, the end of the lightning flash reached all the way to Spoleto, where it entered the infirmary through the window behind my darling's bed. It connected with the dusty machine to which he was wired up, shooting stars like fireworks. Electricity shot down the wires, through the probes, and entered his poor, useless body. Inside, the high voltage raced through his nerves and fused somewhere in his brain, causing a connection that brought him back to life with a jolt. A wisp of smoke came out of the top of his head and the air on the ward was filled with the smell of burning rubber.

Immediately he sat straight up in bed and ripped off the probes that were stuck to his head and body. The moment he had so long prayed for had come suddenly with no warning. If he was dreaming this moment, he would die a million agonizing deaths. As the other patients quaked and gibbered beneath their bedclothes, my heroic Arcadio leapt from the bed and ran along the corridors determined to make straight for Fernanda Ponderosa. Yes, even then, at that defining moment, it lacerates me to report that I did not enter his thoughts.

Wearing nothing but his faded pajamas, he emerged onto the forecourt, snatched a moped then being parked by the night nurse, Carlotta Bolletta, revved up the engine, and roared off in the direction of home. he had never driven before but it didn't matter. He could do anything now. Out on the forecourt, Carlotta Bolletta was left gaping.

The thunder rumbled with each step Primo Castorini took. It was as though his footsteps were responsible for forming it. He had allowed an hour for a journey that took ten minutes. Instead of going slowly, his legs accelerated. He could not hold them back. The journey that should have taken ten minutes took five in these circumstances. The result was he was too early. But the truth was he just couldn't wait any longer. Any suggestion that he could was ridiculous.

Almost at a run he crossed the yard where the eight turtles lay in wait for the rain. They knew it was coming and they would be the first to feel it pattering on their shells. They would feel it gushing through the dry gullies of their wrinkly necks, revitalizing their protruding heads and scaly legs.

The butcher's hair acted as a conduit for all the electrons in the atmosphere, and it seemed more alive now than ever. Or perhaps it was the hormones rampaging within him. Whatever the cause, his hair was ready for the night ahead. So, too, was the rest of him. He was bigger now than usual. He seemed to have grown both taller and broader. The buttons of his shirt were straining. So were the seams of his pants. His body was struggling already to shed its clothes, the way a reptile sheds its skin. He had bounced back from the repression of the preceding weeks that had in a sense shrunk him. Now he was magnificent.

His huge form was silhouetted by the light against the screen door. Like an ogre. Oscar and her babies cowered on the top of the dresser. A turnip moth fluttered around the light, casting a monstrous shadow on the ceiling.

He was early and Fernanda Ponderosa wasn't ready. She was still in the tub, squeezing water from a giant sea sponge over herself. Her hair was caught up in a knot on top of her head, and tender fronds escaped from it, trailing into the foaming water lapping the edge like a tide. She heard the screen door open and shut. Let him come. A coiled thrill unfurled itself in the center of her body. She felt him lumbering around the house like a blind bear, knocking over the furniture, looking for her, scenting her out. She, too, was impatient, but she continued with her bathing ritual, raising each of her legs in turn and applying the frothing sponge to her silver skin. His heavy footfalls were on the stairs. He was coming. She felt a surge of water entering her.

The flickering candlelight drew him at last to the bathroom door, hanging open just wide enough for him to see inside. He stood there, his square shoulders filling the doorframe, uncertain, watching, and although she feigned not to have noticed him, she wanted him to watch her.

Slowly, rhythmically, she allowed the sea sponge to soak up its weight in water, then, lifting it high above her, the excess water tracing the veins in her forearms, she squeezed it out. The expelled water cascaded onto her glistening flesh: her throat, her glorious breasts bobbing up and down, sometimes below the surface of the water, sometimes tantalizingly above it. The sound of water falling into water was all there was in the world.

As he watched, Primo Castorini's mouth went dry. He didn't remember to breathe. He felt like the sponge when it had been wrung out. His body, not his hands, pushed the door open. It couldn't take any more, and it was wise not to. His smell overpowered the perfume of bath oil and unguents: the smoldering musk of pheromones, longing and lust. He came and knelt on the floor beside the tub. He leaned in and began to rescue the rivulets of hair from the water and weave them into the knot on her head. The water soaked up into the cuffs of his shirt, splashed over the rim of the tub onto his chest, and from the floor tiles it permeated the knees of his pants. He was saturated but he didn't notice. The strands of hair defied his attempts to snare them and slipped back silently into the water.

His feral eyes washed over her and his hands followed his eyes. Her wet body was the most sensuous creation imaginable. She lay back with her eyes shut and allowed the most sensitive hands in the region to explore her fully. In future, he never wanted to touch anything that wasn't her. Beneath the water he caressed her, all of her. Instinctively he knew the spots that made her pucker. Her breathing grew heavier and more urgent and he had to hold himself in chains.

Thunderbolts shook the house on its foundations. Lightning cracked, coloring the sky outside green then yellow then red. The storm was directly overhead. Primo Castorini stood up, and in the colored lights that lit up the room, their eyes met and fastened. Was the roar that sounded then the thunder, or did it come from someplace deep inside Primo Castorini? It was difficult to tell.

With one hand he tore off his saturated clothes. They peeled off together, like paper, in one piece. They knew it was futile to resist. Shirt, pants, undershorts, even, amazingly, his socks and shoes. There was to be no scuffling here. No hopping and yanking and cursing and squirming and embarrassment. At what she saw, Fernanda Ponderosa's black eyes widened momentarily. It was the only time she had given anything away. She felt herself being lifted out of the water. She was Aphrodite rising from the waves. The water streamed away from her in rivulets that cascaded onto the floor.

With the sound of artillery, great blistering drops of rain the size of eggs burst on contact with the roof tiles. It was finally raining. And what rain it was.

Primo Castorini carried Fernanda Ponderosa out of the bathroom and into the bedroom.

CHAPTER   FIVE

By some trick of the light the writhing figures of Fernanda Ponderosa and Primo Castorini were magnified to huge proportions and projected through the bedroom window onto the ever-changing canvas of the lowering sky.

Outside, the rain fell in a battery. It hissed onto the parched surfaces and was immediately absorbed. Anyone foolish enough to be out in it suffered blows that left indelible marks on the skin. It was not the benevolent rain the citizens had dreamed of dancing naked in. It was spiteful.

Meanwhile the zombies who had been woken by the white light were making toward the house. The first to arrive was my sweetheart. Without his glasses it was a miracle he arrived at all. The moped had run out of gas two miles back and he had been forced to cover the remaining distance on foot. The great raindrops bit at his face and at his body through the flimsy flannel of his pajamas, but he didn't notice. He was aware of nothing except the thought of Fernanda Ponderosa, which drove him relentlessly onward. He was consumed by a jealousy bigger by far than himself. It dogged his footsteps like an overfed shadow, whispering its poison into his ears, so loud it drowned out the clarion call of the storm. The shadow told him that night he would commit murder. And he believed it.

Fidelio Castorini was making slower progress. His body had suffered during the months he lay dormant in the cave. It was now the body of an old man. The mountain paths and passes made suddenly treacherous by the rain lay in wait for him, and he fell down many times, sustaining terrible injuries.

Arcadio Carnabuci could see nothing clearly, and his eyes were doubly obscured by the rain. He could almost believe the rain was part of the conspiracy against him. The nightmarish quality of the night and the storm was made more nightmarish by his poor eyesight. Monstrous shapes loomed up out of the shadows, terrifying him, and then just as mysteriously, disappeared. Eventually he found the right house. He had been confused by his own cottage not being where he'd left it, but after going round and round in circles, he found the Castorini house, which was in complete darkness, poised between shards of lightning.

As he staggered toward the house, the evil shadow sitting on his shoulder called upon Arcadio to arm himself. A murderer needs a weapon.

"If the pork butcher shows up tonight, he will die," said the gravelly voice.

Nodding as though mesmerized, Arcadio took hold of a large rock he had tripped over in the yard. It was the turtle

Olga, who had been rehydrating herself in a puddle. Quaking, she drew her head, legs, and tail into her shell, offering up a mother's prayer for the safety of her babies.

Lightning irradiated the scene, this time with a yellow glare like mustard gas. In that split second of blinding light, Fidelio Castorini identified his screen door and made toward it. He had come home. Home at last. In that split second of blinding light, Arcadio Carnabuci's eyes focused and he beheld the pork butcher from the rear making toward the house.

"Bingo," cried the voice.

Arcadio Carnabuci's worst fears were confirmed. All the while he had lain in the infirmary, he had been right to fear that evil seducer. He hoped things had not progressed too far in his absence. The butcher had to die. Of that he was certain. It was the only way. In a frenzy he ran forward and smashed the turtle against Fidelio's skull. Fidelio let out an abominable scream. In that scream, magnified above the pandemonium of that clamorous night, was contained all his diabolical anguish at the sudden realization of his plight.

Arcadio Carnabuci, too, tried to scream, but nothing came out. He had lost his voice forever, the one abiding residue of his illness. He would never speak or sing again. The form of the pork butcher fell back onto Arcadio, causing him to try to scream again. Or perhaps he had not stopped trying to scream throughout. Who can tell?

Lightning struck again and this time the light stayed on, green and lurid, and by it Arcadio saw his mistake. It was not the pork butcher at all. For all their figures were exactly the same from the back view, from the front they were different. This character had a bushy beard grown down to his knees. A shock of hair like a bush. Admittedly the pork butcher had a shock of hair, but it was mild in comparison with this. And from his mouth from which a trickle of blood was flowing were great fanglike teeth that struck more terror into Arcadio Carnabuci's soul than anything else.

Fernanda Ponderosa and Primo Castorini in a brief lull between their seventh and eighth bouts of lovemaking heard the scream ripping apart the night. Primo Castorini was all for carrying on regardless, but Fernanda Ponderosa sensed tragedy and hurried to dress in spite of his attempts to stop her. So he, too, threw open the closet and pulled on some of his brother's things that hung there still.

The rain suddenly stopped, leaving the air fresh and cool. The thunder had rumbled away over the mountains, and the sky remained lit as bright as day.

The breathless lovers appeared on the scene of the carnage at precisely the same moment as I galloped into the yard with my mistress clinging to my back. We were followed by roaring sirens heralding the arrival of a truckload of officers of the carabinieri, and the ambulance driven by Irina Biancardi, supported by Gianluigi Pupini.

My darling, still screaming a silent scream, looked deranged, particularly when he witnessed the all too obvious state of relations between she whom he persisted in regarding as his future bride, and the pork butcher, who was all too much alive.

"Fidelio," roared Primo Castorini, recognizing his brother in spite of his lupine appearance, and throwing himself on his knees beside the body.

"Silvana," murmured Fidelio at the sight of Fernanda Ponderosa. Then with his last breath he added, "I love you," and promptly died.

Olga the turtle, who had sustained horrific injuries, died also, leaving seven orphans.

The yard was suddenly full of people. Our grapevine is more efficient than that of any other region, and our citizens are not slow to heed its call. Some were wearing pajamas and nightgowns, although most were wearing very little, having cast off their sleepwear long ago on account of the heat. A murder usually brings people together, especially when it happens on your own doorstep. There had never been such a feeling of camaraderie amongst the citizens, who were usually quick to stab one another in the back.

"Arcadio Carnabuci a murderer! Who'd have believed it, eh?"

"Always thought he was an odd one."

"What a lucky escape we have had, neighbors."

"Praise be."

There was a ripple of excitement as my beloved was placed in handcuffs. I tried to make my way over to him, to comfort him, but I, too, was tethered, by means of a rope. Although my eyes were glued to him, and full of love, he had eyes only for Fernanda Ponderosa, who had eyes only for Primo Castorini. Speranza Patti, wearing a nightgown far too revealing for a woman of her age and avoirdupois, looked dewy-eyed at my darling, and had I not been tethered, I would most certainly have given her a nasty nip on the rump with my teeth.

While the body of Fidelio Castorini, who had come back from the dead only to die once more, was being placed in the ambulance, my darling's legs were frog-marching him away amid those of two young officers clad in tight pants with a wide red stripe running down the side. He was bundled into the rear of the official vehicle, the door slammed before being padlocked, and his only view of the outside world was through the bars at the tiny window, which revealed a glimpse of Speranza Patti mouthing the words:

"I'll wait for you. Forever."

If only I could have got free of that rope.

CHAPTER SIX

The cataclysmic storm had restored the region to its usual balance. The sun was benevolent, not blistering, and was already packing for its winter vacation. The rumbles beneath the earth ceased, and we no longer feared an earthquake. Grass grew green again, not brown. The animals rehydrated. Sheep shed their blue coats, revealing fluffy white ones underneath. Goats and cows began to give milk again. Cheese makers the length and breadth of the region could start curding cheese again. Moles started digging. Rats started gnawing. Bees buzzed. Birds sang. Water ran through the rivers and streams and waterfalls. The lake had filled and the swans were swimming on it. Speckled trout stuck out their rubber lips and snatched at the flies who were again flying.

The residents were able to conduct their regular business. All those except Luigi Bordino. The morning found him dead, and Susanna refusing to meet her husband's eye. The corpse was discovered with its head submerged in a basin of pear-flavored dough that was to have been shaped into a tasty treat for Fernanda Ponderosa. Susanna insisted he had been struck by lightning, but Melchiore was not so sure. Already, high-technology electric ovens were being installed in the bakery, and sign writers were at work transforming the frontage. *Susanna Bordino* was written there large in a curly calligraphic script. It was as though Luigi Bordino had never existed. Yet she had committed the murder unnecessarily.

I drew the cart, festooned with white ribbons and rosebuds, containing the blushing newlyweds Concetta and Amilcare Croce home to their cottage in the Via Alfieri. On the way I passed Sancio, the Castorini mule, who was tethered outside the Happy Pig, munching on a leaf of fresh green fern. He gave me one look with his slow eyes and I was smitten. I burned with a love the like of which I had never known. In that instant of revelation I understood the universe. I had never loved Arcadio Carnabuci. It had all been a terrible mistake. It was Sancio I loved, and in his eyes I read that my love was returned.

Tearing my eyes away from my new and tender love, I noticed the town library was closed up. Speranza Patti had followed Arcadio Carnabuci to the district capital, where she was exploiting her civil service connections and was busy making representations on his behalf at the highest level. She would never give up on her mission to clear his name and secure his release from the *carcere*. Languishing in his cell, Arcadio Carnabuci had realized his fatal mistake. The woman of his dreams was not Fernanda Ponderosa. It was Speranza Patti.

He had got their names muddled. What a fool he had been. A complete and utter fool.

Fernanda Ponderosa did not appear for work that day at the Happy Pig. A line was waiting outside before Primo Castorini had even rolled up the shutter and raised the blinds that shaded the window. Pucillo's Pork Factory had been decimated by a thunderbolt the previous night, and now that the temperature had dropped, everybody in the region was craving ham. Primo Castorini worked mechanically. His mind was saturated by Fernanda Ponderosa. He felt guilty, knowing he should be mourning his brother's death, but he reasoned he had mourned him once already. He could still smell Fernanda Ponderosa on his skin. Every so often a microscopic bubble of the aroma they had made together would burst somewhere about him and the vapor would carry to his nose. At such times he would groan loudly in remembered ecstasy, causing the ham-buying public to nod indulgently and wink and nudge one another with their elbows. He replayed incessantly every moment of the night. He relived each extraordinary orgasm. He could not stop his lips from smiling, and he didn't want to.

But then a fear began to gnaw away at him. He couldn't bear to be without her. He had come on ahead. She was supposed to follow. Where was she? He felt a sense of panic. He couldn't explain it. Then he realized it was love. He had never felt it before. And he felt like singing. Then he wore out his watch by looking at it. Anytime now she would come. But she didn't.

In the midst of serving the legions of customers that besieged the shop, he knew he had to go to her, right then. He had been stupid not to do it before. He had wasted a whole hour of being with her. An hour he would never get back. He was furious with himself. So he just walked away, leaving them to it. The citizens looked at one another blankly, then began helping themselves to the hams. Soon the thieving Nellinos were loading up a truck with them.

The five minutes of the journey to the house were the longest in Primo Castorini's life. He felt fear, certainly. All lovers are frightened. It's a big part of the job. He also felt the most terrible impatience to be with her. Hold her. Bury himself in her. Inhale her scent. Kiss her endlessly. Caress her body. Drown in her. Then he was seized by the fear again, only worse this time. She had gone. That's why she hadn't come to the shop. She had left him. Disappeared. And he would never see her again. A great echoing chasm of terror opened up inside his body. How could he bear it?

He approached the old house at a run. He saw a moving van parked out in the yard. Men were loading it with unicorns, chandeliers, statues, grandfather clocks, banana trees, oak chests, and all kinds of stuff. He saw it but he didn't allow himself to accept it. His starving eyes sought her out, panic rising in them like a tide. She had gone. She really had gone.

No. She was here. She was still here. She hadn't gone. It was all right. Everything was all right again. His heart expanded, causing a sharp pain that shot like an arrow through his chest.

That morning Fernanda Ponderosa had said her final good-byes to Silvana, and although she had hoped her sister might have one last kind word for her in parting, once more she was met with silence. She accepted now without bitterness that Silvana had been right all along: death couldn't make everything right between them; it couldn't change a single thing.

Now she was bending beneath the fig tree, smoothing earth over the grave of the turtle. The pork butcher ran to her and swept her up into his arms and held her there forever, or at least for a long, long time, until the slightest constriction of the muscles of her body made him reluctantly replace her feet on the ground.

Her eyes wouldn't tell him anything. But the sane part of him knew the answers, and he hated that part, wished he could rip it out of him and throttle it. Long ago she had said she would stay until Fidelio came back. He had come. And now she was leaving. That was all. She stroked his cheek with her fingertips and walked over to the van, which was all packed up and waiting to go. He knew he could do nothing to make her stay. He would do anything. But it wasn't enough.

"Where are you going?" He was surprised at the sound of his voice. It sounded the way it usually did. Almost.

The driver started the engine.

"A lot of questions," she replied with half a smile. And he had to watch as the truck bumped across the yard, turned into the lane, and drove away.

"Only one," he managed. But she had gone.